C000319900

# DEATH HEAD
# VALLEY

## DAVID CHARLESWORTH

Published in Great Britain in 2019 by
Hellbound Media
an independent publisher

*www.hellboundmedia.co.uk*

Copyright © 2019 David Charlesworth

Cover by David V G Davies
(www.FTS-ltd-UK.com)

Back Cover Photo by Magnus Claren
(www.facebook.com/magnus.claren.photography)

ISBN- 978-0-9934266-7-4

Set in Garamond

First Edition

This book is dedicated to anyone keeping the slasher genre alive: Fans, artists, film-makers, and game-developers.

You are the lightning that brings the resurrection.

The rain hammered down with such force that Artie had to physically stiffen his neck in order to keep his view straight. He'd never experience weather this shitty before and he prayed to God he never would again.

His hat, touted as waterproof, was living up to the promise made by the eager clerk at the camping store... his slacks, however, were another story. He could feel the damp pool that had gathered in the indent his backside made in the fishing chair and it was starting to wrinkle his balls and ass. *That's all I need.* He thought to himself. *Another reason for Wanda to avoid looking at me in the bedroom.*

Behind him, rummaging through the car was Todd. Even over the sound of the thundering river and the accompanying roar of the storm Artie could hear him singing to himself.

'Asshole.' He spat.

He hated fishing. He hated camping. He hated being outdoors. Why the hell did he even agree to this? Todd was adamant that they do something over the weekend. He insisted they get out and away from their usual haunts: The usual bars, the play-offs, *their wives.* But why fishing?

Wanda wasn't best pleased that Artie had been passed over for promotion again. Though they both knew that was just a convenient, on-hand excuse for yet another argument. A divorce was looming on the horizon, haunting their relationship and they were both prodding each other, pushing each other to step closer towards saying those inevitable words and making it a reality. How fishing was meant to help with that was beyond Artie's understanding.

Todd came waddling past. 'Sure is a doozy, huh?' he said.

'Sure is,' Artie replied, trying, and failing, to hide his contempt. He gazed at the line. He didn't know the tensile strength of it, nor did he know what bait was attached to the hook, nor the lure used, but his rod was pulled left as the river rushed past. There was a million to one chance of a fish swimming into his hook, he guessed. It'd have to be gawping at *exactly* the right time, at *exactly* the right angle and going at *exactly* the right speed. He had a better chance of reconciling things with Wanda.

Although, according to Todd on their ride here, *"catching a fish is the least interesting part of fishing!"*

Beside him, Todd began setting up his gear. His rainproof coat and slacks were huge and puffy and made his proportions look like that of a toddler's. He awkwardly fixed his chair and slumped into it, arms jutting out to the sides. Artie saw the flaw in his plan immediately, but said nothing. Of all the things to forget, Todd had sat down without the most important thing a fisherman might need... his rod. He glanced to his sides twice before it sank in. 'God damn it all!' he cried out.

'Hey, I thought catching the fish was the worst part of all this?' Artie gloated.

'Yeah, well... I still want the *illusion* of being able to

catch one. Smart-ass.'

The giant man-child struggled to his feet, his bulk a hindrance when it came to finer motor functions, and slipped off behind them. Their setup was illuminated by a high powered halogen light they'd set up and Artie's shadow reached out, long and low across the rapid torrents and onto the far bank. The light was so strong it even caught the opposing tree line.

As Todd passed by the lamp he threw the world into darkness for the briefest of seconds. When the light came back Artie felt a clench in his chest as something (or *someone*) he hadn't registered before ducked back into the dense woods opposite.

'Fuck me... Todd?' he called out. Keeping his eyes fixed on the dark shadows across the way, peering through the haze of rain that made the whole world look like one of the badly tuned *"stag"* video tapes him and his pals used to watch as kids when his folks were out of the house. He shifted slightly, soaking even more of his undercarriage as the water that pooled there sluiced around his butt.

*He was a city boy.* He insisted to himself once again. *He wasn't one for the countryside, why was he here?* Even when he married Wanda their honeymoon had been to Vegas. One huge, massive city. *They could have gone camping outside of Vegas! At least it'd be dry!*

'Todd?' he called again. God only knew what was out there in the dark, skulking in the shadows: bears, wolves or worse... he'd seen Deliverance. Todd may have looked more like Ned Beatty than he did, but Todd also boxed in his college years and kept it up as a lark every few weeks. What could he do if some mutated hick came for him, lust in their inbred eyes and hands on their weapons? Offer to do their taxes?

It was too much and he all but screamed, *'TODD!'*

'What?' the lumbering hulk asked, as he crossed back over the light. The world vanished for a blink, and Artie could have swore he saw *it* again, but back in the company of his friend he felt the fool and could not bring himself to admit his fears.

'Thought I had a bite,' he lied.

Todd fell back into his chair, rod by his side and a beer in his hand. Water splashed out from under him. He clearly bought the right pants and didn't care where he sat. He necked the beer back, rain slathering his face and Artie had to wonder how much of what his pal had swallowed was booze and what was filthy rainwater.

'Isn't this just the life?' Todd said, beaming.

'It's something alright,' Artie grumbled.

'Me and my Daddy used to come up these ways all the time when I was a boy. Fishing, hunting, camping... you name it.'

Artie wanted to add something about being corn-holed by hillbillies, but kept his mouth shut.

'Shame he ain't with us any more,' Todd continued, 'I think you woulda liked him.'

'Yeah? Why's that?' Artie asked.

'Because he was a miserable prick too!' Todd laughed, 'But no, seriously... I wish I could have brought him back up here. Hell, I wish I would have come back up here sooner too. The nostalgia is incredible. The smells, the sights, the sounds...'

'So why did you stop? What changed?'

'Ah, there was that shit with those kids,' Todd said, killing his beer.

'What kids?' Artie asked, shifting himself to get a better look at his buddy. Todd was staring out across the far bank, his eyes had glazed over.

'See, there's a quarry up the way there and there was a small community that was built up around it as well as the actual town down the way. We used to come in and meet the locals and have a grand old time of it. I was about sixteen or so when it happened... There was a big accident. A lot of people died and over the next few years the valley kinda grew sour. The locals, with no trade, began to disperse or try and tough it out. That's when the first kid died.'

'Note the way I said *first* kid. They'd either turn up dead or go missing. Soon the valley got a nasty reputation and my Daddy said it just wasn't the place he'd grew up with, y'know? I didn't pay much mind to it, as callous as that sounds. Kids went missing, turned up dead, but no foul play was called. But either way, without him pulling me along I just stopped coming here too. I was more interested in chicks then... and cars... and doing things to chicks *in* cars, if you know what I mean.'

'Kids died?' Artie repeated, 'What happened to them then if it wasn't foul play?'

Todd didn't reply, just kept his gaze fixed on the far bank. Artie didn't realise it, but his questions had been whispered and didn't carry to his friend's ears. They sat, silent amidst the storm when suddenly Todd flinched.

'AW SHIT!' he cried out, and Artie's heart nearly leapt from his throat at the outburst, 'forgot my damn tackle box!'

Todd did his usual pantomime of getting out of his chair and stomped back towards the car, blocking out the light again and though there were no shifting figments of his imagination this time he could have swore the far shadows were darker than they had been a few moments ago.

'Christ,' he grumbled, 'fishing in god damn haunted

woods. Why couldn't his Pa have gotten him into something other than this nature shit. Like strip clubs or golf.'

The rain continued to pummel his head and he let his neck give, slumping forward, his spirit trampled by the horrific truth of his surroundings. Now he had to worry about inbred hillbillies *killing* him as well as violating him. Just great!

His hand, still firmly on his rod, didn't even register the unusual twitching at first, not until a fierce yank nearly took it right out from between his fingers. Something was pulling on the line, something stronger than the usual pull of the river.

'You have GOT to be kidding me!' he laughed.

A bite! A million to one chance and he'd gotten it! He strengthened his grip on the rod and began to reel in the line as a shadow was cast over him, plunging the world into darkness.

'I GOT A BITE, TODD! I GOT A GOD DAMNED BITE! WHO SAYS LANDING A FISH IS THE LEAST INTERESTING PART?'

In the darkness he continued to reel in his quarry, fighting the pull like Todd had told him to, and his heart was near fit to burst from his rib cage. He'd never felt so alive! Maybe Todd knew what he was talking about after all. A million to one chance of landing a bite. A million to one chance of making his marriage work again. All of a sudden he liked those odds!

'Todd, buddy. Get out of the light for me? I can't see what I'm doing!'

Light flooded the area again and out of Artie's peripheral vision he saw something land in Todd's chair with a wet smack. He glanced at it for all of a second before looking back at the line... *What was that?* he thought, his mind fighting against the obvious and horrifying truth.

He looked again and forgot all about the reel. The fish took off, taking with it the lure, and the line quickly ran out and snapped. Artie didn't care though as he could not take his eyes from what had been dumped into the chair besides him.

Todd's dead eyes stared back at him, rainwater pooling in them as well as his mouth, which was frozen open in a silent scream. The fabric of the chair was beginning to stain red where blood ran from Todd's neck which had been savagely hacked from his body.

Artie's jaw dropped as he matched Todd's expression. They both looked just like a fish hooked on a line: Eyes wide, mouth agape, unable to comprehend what was happening.

Artie began to scream and put all of his joking aside; What were the odds of *actually* getting murdered in the woods? *Really?*

He turned into the light and saw the flash of an axehead as it came flying towards him in a large, overhead arc.

A million to one, surely!

# 1.

It was like a postcard, Annie thought, as the final straggling remnants of the storm slipped away revealing the true splendour of the twin mountain peaks of Alan and Allan. They appeared to have erupted from the ground at their own volition in what was otherwise a flat state, and it was there, nestled in their shadowy basin that they were planning to spend the weekend.

The plains and farmland were covered with glistening dew that was drying under the now-baking summer sun, making the grass and wheat sparkle as it rippled like calm ocean waves.

The smell of the fields swamped the car, that fresh *green* smell you never found in the city. She lowered her window all the way down and let the aroma fuel the buzzing energy that had been building in her stomach. She could not sit still, she felt like a kid going to Disneyland, but she refused to give in and dance along to the cheesy Eighties pop music Donovan was playing on the radio. She'd swore that she'd *never* dance to the old man music he liked.

Instead, she stuck her head out of the window and

let the hot winds whip through her golden locks that trailed behind her as though she were underwater.

'You part dog?' Donovan said, reaching over and gently pinching her side,

She let out a little scream, 'Asshole!' and smacked him away, but he didn't hear her, the wind took her words away before they reached his ears. And though he had not heard her, he met her eyes regardless and they shared a smile. His teeth were bright and brilliant, even in the relative gloom of the SUV. That perfect smile on that perfect face. She had to be the luckiest person alive to be with Donovan Rooney, the most wonderful person alive.

Annie had known she had fallen in love the exact moment he had quit football to be with her.

The coach and the rest of the team had kittens when he broke the news. It was the last year of college and they were just a few months away from the big game and there were rumours that professional scouts would be there.

*"Practice is getting in the way of the best years of our lives,"* he'd said to her, *"What are the odds of going pro anyway? And if I did, that would mean more practice. More time apart. If there's even a one percent chance that I'd lose you because of that, then it's not a bet I'd be willing to take."*

That was the night of their first barbecue, something that had become a yearly celebration. Hence the trip. It began as an act of defiance, promising to only love and live for themselves and by their own means from there on out... and they had. The gang had split and gone their separate ways without any arguments or vitriol, and their yearly get-togethers were now a celebration of their friendship as they chased their own dreams. Though whether they would ever catch them was a different matter altogether.

The bright green plains took on darker hues as trees

began to dot the landscape. The woodlands began to take precedence as the mountains drew ever nearer.

As Annie slipped back into the car a voice called out from the back seat, 'Aw man!'

She craned her neck to look at *"their"* Philly. He was cramped away in the corner besides the camping gear, head buried in his phone, more comfortable in the virtual world that he ever was in the real one. He was holding his cell up to the window, then he tried holding it out to his side. Every movement was awkward and he constantly bumped his hand against parts of the car.

'What's up?' she asked.

He glanced up with his nervous eyes, 'No signal. I thought you said they had a cell tower here?'

'No, I said they were *building* a cell tower here,' Donovan said.

'Well are they going to have it up in the next three minutes?'

'Maybe? I guess we'll find out in four.'

'Dang.'

Annie kept her eyes on her Philly. His head twitched back and forth and she stifled a giggle as he looked more like a bird than ever. A big owl's head on a gangly rake of a body.

There was no two ways about it, their friendship was a complete and utter fluke, but it was a mistake they were all glad had been made.

For extra credit Philly had signed up for an after school class, but misread the flyer and thought he was going to be studying *video games* and instead wound up in a biology club about *viral germs*. Being young (and by his own admission, a complete loser) he stayed for the entire hour out of fear of appearing the fool and admitting he came to the wrong study room. The session ended and he left without much fanfare, only for the strangest thing to happen... come the following week, he turned up again. Exactly the same mistake, exactly the same nervous dedication to not wanting to stand out and be noticed. Annie had been partnered with the odd duck then and, wouldn't you know it, they'd made each other laugh.

What followed was a peculiar few months where she could have swore Philly was harbouring a crush, but the more he hung out with herself and Donovan the closer they grew. Don especially enjoyed his company, bonding over their shared love for trashy horror movies and a love for the supernatural, despite it freaking Philly out.

He began to relax, started speaking up around crowds and eased up on falling in love with every girl who gave him the time of day. Well... all but one.

He was still a huge dork, but he was *their* dork.

'Why are you so desperate for a signal anyway?' Annie asked, fearing the response, 'we not good enough company for you all of a sudden?'

'You're fine company... barely,' he said with a smile, 'I was texting Zoe.'

And there it was. Philly's Achilles heel. Annie glanced at Donovan who just shrugged and they let the conversation drop. After what happened last year they decided it was best not to poke that hornet's nest and just crossed their fingers and hoped for the best.

A sliver of grey on the horizon heralded the arrival of the small town, on the cusp of the woods at the base of the mountains, and Duran Duran started up on the radio. The thought of anything other than this being the start of the greatest weekend of the year slipped effortlessly from Annie's mind and the buzz in her stomach ballooned and she caught herself nodding along to the music.

'Just give in and dance,' Donovan said, slapping the wheel in tune to *Planet Earth*.

So she did.

Donovan dropped a hand from the wheel and slid it into his pocket and he was *certain* she knew. He felt the band, his Mom's wedding ring that was held tight to his leg by his jeans. He was an idiot, jeopardising the surprise by touching it when he could feel it pressing against his thigh anyway. It was all his brain could register, that small lump against his leg. He could not help it though. It felt unreal, like this was someone else's dream and if they woke up the ring would vanish.

Tomorrow. He planned to do it tomorrow. They'd go for a little drive through the valley and find a picturesque area and he'd take to one knee. It was a shame his Pop couldn't be there. If Donovan didn't know his old man any better he'd swear his Pop was about to shed a tear when he had asked if he could use his Mom's ring to propose.

The scattered remnants of the town of *Angélique* began to pass them by. Homes long since abandoned and boarded up sat in yards where the grass and plant life had took dominion, ready to thoroughly reclaim the land that man had so arrogantly built on.

Rotting bunting hung on rusted, twisted wires that stretched from the old sodium street lights that lined the main strip; relics from a time where every day was a celebration of prosperity. They were joined by old flags, faded and dirty that flapped from their poles affixed to buildings that once housed stores and cafes. Much like the homes they passed the store fronts were boarded up, and broken windows hid the shame of the gutted innards of once proud businesses.

The gang looked up, past these hollow shells that lay dark and dormant, and up at the mountain faces of the two Alans' that sat in watch, blotting out most of the sky.

'It'd be pretty majestic if this wasn't a ghost town,' Philly said.

They slowed to a near crawl, taking in the view.

'Been this was since the fifties, I think,' Donovan said,

He'd done some light reading about the place before they came. Specifically checking the Google Maps aerial images to see if there was any good vantage points within the valley itself. There was no official name for the valley but it had garnered the nickname *Death Head Valley*. Mostly from the way the two dark mountains appeared like eye sockets and the town spread out in an upside down V shape looked like the empty nasal cavity. He'd saved a picture to his phone to bust out around the campfire later. He was looking forward to freaking Philly out with it.

The strip ended at a wall of trees and with it, civilization ended too. The trees made up the woods that carpeted the valley floor between the mountains and a dirt trail cut into them and ran parallel to a river that ran off to their right and under an old, iron bridge. Before it sat the only two buildings that appeared to have survived the depression: a dive bar and a grubby looking diner.

An old guy pushed his way out from the gloom of the bar, passing by a burnt out sign for Coors, and blinked his tiny eyes as he looked at that SUV, as if he didn't quite believe what he was seeing. Then, much to the horror of Annie and Philly, Donovan pulled up and lowered his window.

'What the hell are you doing?' Annie hissed, afraid the old drunk might hear her.

'Just drive on!' Philly urged.

'It's alright, it's O.K,' Donovan cooed.

The old man pulled his stained cap down over his eyes which were red and clearly not used to seeing natural daylight. He approached the vehicle with slow, measured steps. Each footfall threatening to send him tumbling.

'You goin' the valley?' he said, voice hoarse, each syllable coming out hard.

'Yes sir,' Donovan said, 'just a couple of days, that's all. Do we have to inform the Sheriff or-'

'You can't go into them woods. Stay out of the valley, hear?'

'Is it privately owned? That's why I pulled over to ask if-'

'Only person who owns them woods is Connor Finlayson!' The old man cut in. He stepped forward a few more paces, his eyes were now wide and wild, his voice softened, and now the words came easily as he continued his rant, 'I'm *begging* you kids, don't go in there. People stay out of the valley ever since the quarry accident. Only person to survive was Connor. Saw his whole family die as a boy, drove him mad. Now he kills whoever comes into the valley as revenge...'

'Donovan, dude...' Philly urged from the back seat.

Behind the old man a flat face, built like a bulldog's, was peering out from the window of the diner. Its owner was small but heavily set and wore a ratty brown uniform. She shook her head before silently calling out to someone they couldn't see.

'There's nothing but death in the valley, kids,' the old drunk continued, 'people go into the valley and go missing, turn up dead... Please for the love of all that's good in the world. Please-'

'*JIMMY!*' A voice called out.

The diner's door was thrown open. A man with a heavy moustache and cheeks thick with stubble was marching towards them. His hair was oiled back and glistened in the late afternoon sun.

'Maisie has some coffee in the pot for you. You go on inside now,' he said.

'Franco, you can't let these kids go into the woods. Tell them, Francis. *Please!*'

'Nothing wrong with the woods, Jimmy. You know that,' he then turned to the car and repeated, 'Nothing wrong with the valley, folks.'

'Nobody comes out of there alive! So many people have gone missing! We can't let Connor keep getting away with this!'

Maisie, the waitress, had joined the fray. She smiled at the group, a forced turning up of the lips. A smile that never met her eyes, as Donovan's mom used to say. He understood what that meant now. Though he couldn't blame the woman. She lived in a town with barely one final breath left in it, after all.

'You kids want some pie?' she asked, placing a thick arm around Jimmy's shoulder, guiding him away. The old man sank into himself, his fight gone. 'Jimmy here'll sit quietly in the corner, wontcha, Jim. I know the old place don't look like much, but the food is real good. Believe you me!'

'We're meeting friends, but thank you anyway,' Annie said.

Maisie smiled again and began to walk Jimmy back.

'If you get tired of eatin' your store bought burgers just remember we're only down the road. Take care now.'

As she left, Francis leant in, placing his hands on the roof of the truck. His breath was heavy with the smell of coffee, its stink just about hid the reek of whiskey, 'Sorry about Jimmy there. Lost his kids, shook him up something awful... didn't lose them in the valley, mind. I've been going out hog hunting with nothing but my spears for as long as I can recall. Just to keep their numbers down, you understand. Valley's a beautiful place and we're proud of it. Nothing wrong out there. Just been some... unfortunate circumstances is all.'

'Thanks for letting us know,' Donovan said, 'so we don't need permission to camp at all?'

'Not as far as I'm aware. Not heading in *too* deep, right? No mountain rescue here in town and as I say, real easy to have an accident out there.'

'No, nothing wild. We've been camping and hiking for a few years now. Fully stocked with first aid kits, clean water and we know which berries not to eat.'

'We're just looking to roast some marshmallows and watch the stars. That sort of thing,' Annie smiled.

'Yeah sure!' Francis laughed. 'As well as getting' fucked up and then getting fucked, right?'

'WHOAH! Hey now!' Donovan shouted, leaning out towards Francis.

'Jesus Christ!' Philly cried out.

'Easy. Easy...' Francis said, raising his arms in mock surrender. 'Didn't just mean your lady there, I meant the whole bunch of you. I know what kids are like. That's all. Say, you want me to bring some extra booze along? Some pills? Maybe we can kick things up a notch, know what I mean?'

'Oh God! Just drive, Donny,' Annie said, turning away.

Donovan stared at the guy for a moment. He wanted to get out and put his fist though his smug face and he would have done it as well. But Annie placed her hand on his, calming him. He'd spent a lot of his youth fighting, it made him a natural on the football field, but it also caused him more trouble than it was worth at times. He pushed out the thoughts of busting open the perverts face and, in response, he put his foot down, the truck roaring away, across the road and onto the dark trail. Franco's laughter following them until all trace of the vile man, and civilization, was swallowed up by the woods.

# 2.

Within the valley sat a raised hillock of clear and flat ground. Upon it Bilbo was re-checking his camping supplies. The fire pit itself had been set in the middle of the clearing, naturally. He had set up the protective ring of rocks around it and erected the free standing grill across the flames. Around that, sat the chairs, his being at least four times the size of everyone else's. Bilbo was near enough four hundred pounds and required a specialist, reinforced quasi hammock to support his massive bulk.

They had parked down the embankment, just inside the treeline and the gentle walk up to where he was now had nearly killed him. That's why he was adamant about making sure everything was in order. No way in hell was he heading back down to the *"car park"* again until it was time to leave.

Besides his gargantuan chair, in coolers and containers were everything he'd need for the weekend: Drinks (alcoholic and soda), snacks, real food, blankets because he planned to sleep out under the stars one night, and most importantly, an absurdly large amount of marijuana.

He sat down and let out a grateful sigh. If things went to plan he'd not need to move again until his bladder was full. He leant over to his left and grabbed a beer, then to his right to pick up a freshly constructed joint.

It was glorious!

Probably his finest work to date. He held it out in his palm and felt the weight of it. He had constructed it using almost a whole pack of rolling papers and it was enough to feed a family of four, it was his warm up for the weekend. He sparked the beast and brought the roach to his eager lips, stopping for just a moment to appreciate the aroma. It was strong and sweet and brought a tear to his eye.

'This is the motherfuckin' life,' he said, taking a drag.

And that was Bilbo. A simple man who enjoyed the simple things. People who didn't know him would call him lazy and disgusting; wondering how someone could let themselves get so fat. The truth was not that Bilbo didn't care, it was that Bilbo was completely and utterly at peace with himself. He enjoyed what he enjoyed: weed, good company, and fantasy in the forms of books, films, and video games. In fact, the nickname Bilbo had begun as an insult in high school. But Brendan, as he was then, loved it. Already a chubby kid with a heart for adventure (not literally, though, as it would be likely to explode under too much duress) he wore the Hobbit moniker with pride. He had even wanted to go and get his name changed officially, but that would mean waiting in a queue in some office somewhere, probably. And he argued with himself that he hadn't time for that. Especially seeing as he had just started a new game of *Skyrim*.

He kept in a lungful of smoke before exhaling the thick, hazy cloud and wondered what Kevin and the new kid, (*what was his name? Antony?*) were up to. He began to daydream about the woods and the adventures they might have gone on, just like his namesake. The babbling brooks, the glades and dales, the secret grottos of the world. He scanned the trees and imagined giant, walking trees, Ents, out there. Kevin and Anton (*that was it*) being carried around by sentient Firs and Redwoods.

As much as he would have loved to have joined them, his imagination was as good as, in his mind. Real life could offer only so much, after all. He'd tried to explain his dreams and ideas to Kevin a few times, but he'd always miss out key details or get the sequence of events mixed up and in the end the pair of them would just end up falling about laughing at the nonsense Bilbo had just spewed. And that was just fine for Bilbo. So long as his friend was happy.

The buzz had wrapped him up nicely now. His mind was padded and chill. He reached down and grabbed himself a packet of chips as, on the verge of his senses, he heard the hum of an engine and the grinding drone of wheels on soil. That had to be Annie and Donovan, and his little homie Philly. From his low profile he couldn't see the car, but he could tell it had driven past where they had parked up. Then the top of the vehicle crept into view...

He spat out his joint in a fit of coughing and spluttering.

It was a police cruiser and it was stalking up towards him at a deliberately slow pace! He quickly shifted to try and stamp out his masterpiece and failed, his thick thighs getting in the way of each other. Then he tried to reach down to pick it up to stash it in his open can, but his gut halted his attempts. It was too late anyway, he heard the cop's door open and then slam close. He was busted!

'Howdy,' the cop called out. His voice entirely pleasant.

'Hey man... I mean hello officer,' Bilbo replied, trying to waft away the smell of weed by pretending to stretch. He caught sight of the officer's badge. The Sheriff didn't move, but he was built like a linebacker and had a square, cleanly shaven jaw. His hair was hidden under his hat, but Bilbo figured if it was blonde he may as well have been speaking to Captain America. O.K maybe Captain America's middle aged uncle.

'Name's Montrose,' the Sheriff said.

'Pleasure to meet you, sir. I'm Bilb... Brendan Washington.'

Perhaps he hadn't noticed the joint and the wind had carried away the smell of weed. Bilbo's gut clenched as Montrose approached. Then he took off his hat, revealing hair that was smartly cut and disappointingly brown.

'Having a good time smoking out here?' he said.

He *was* busted. For the first time in his life he felt something akin to fear. First of all what would these people out here even do with a black guy for smoking weed, then, worse still, what would his Mom say? It'd break her heart.

'It's uh, medicinal, sir. I have papers for it... but they're at home.'

'That right, huh?' Montrose said, face blank and impassive, before slowly his lips cracked into a smirk, 'Weed is legal in this state. But from the look on your face, you didn't know that, huh?'

'I near had a heart attack there!' Bilbo laughed.

'Sorry about that,' Montrose said, laughing too, 'just couldn't resist. I know the ideas people have about us small town cops. They see Rambo once and think we're all hard-ass bastards who just want to bust a strangers chops. It's just the opposite in fact. We so rarely get visitors the last thing I want to do is have them leaving with a poor opinion of our little part of this big old world. So how's it going? The whole camping thing?'

'Pretty good thanks, Sheriff...' Bilbo relaxed and reached for his lost spliff. After a few lunges Montrose strode over, plucked it from the ground and passed it back to him.

'Thank you. Couple of my boys have gone out exploring, few more people coming later.'

'Just here for the weekend?'

'Yeah. Maybe Tuesday. Depends on what runs out first, toilet paper or beer.'

Sheriff Montrose smiled and replaced his hat, 'Great stuff. Hey, listen. I won't stick around and put anyone else off having a good time. You've obviously got your head on straight, so can I just rattle off some general guidelines and can you relay them to your friends?'

Bilbo nodded as his thought drifted slightly. Were Sheriff's just modern day paladins? Were forest rangers just modern day rangers?

'Well, first of all, with the river and the mountains the area never gets *too* dry. We don't usually have much call for worrying about fires. But all the same-'

'Only *I* can prevent them,' Bilbo cut in, quoting Smokey the Bear, then held his hand up in salute, 'sorry for butting in, Officer. Used to be a Scout.'

'Excellent! Good to hear it. Then the next thing shouldn't be an issue either. For the moment the valley isn't registered land, but all the same we have a lot of pride for what we have here despite...' He paused and cleared his throat. 'Despite what happened. We'd really appreciate it if you cleared up after yourselves. No garbage or non bio-degradable junk.'

'Of course, Sheriff.' What did he mean by *"what happened"*, that didn't sound good. Not at all. Bilbo was about to ask, but Montrose hadn't stopped his speech,

'Just one last thing... I don't want to sour your weekend, but someone else is in the valley with you. Passed through a couple of days ago. Didn't stop, didn't say hello, and I couldn't find him out here. He looked pretty... *intense...* is the word I'd use. Now, I wouldn't get *too* worried. We often get campers out here who just want to keep to themselves and this guy was in a nice enough truck. I don't think you've got Charles Manson for a neighbour, but all the same I wanted to let you know. You're not alone out here.'

Bilbo's mouth dropped as the Sheriff nodded as he tweaked his hat and sauntered back to his car.

*Not alone?* Christ, what kind of parting words were those? And what kind of bad history did this place have? And where exactly were Kevin and Anton?

# 3.

Kevin's hands were shaking so bad he was afraid to take them out of his pockets lest Anton see them and make fun of him. He'd never done anything nearly this crazy or wild before and there Anton was, calm as anything as though nothing had happened. *Anton is the coolest.* He thought to himself, fretting that he'd accidentally said it out loud. Kevin wanted to ask if Anton had his goatee and long hair in order to look more like Satan. But he figured that was a dumb question and didn't want to insult his new friend. Anton was a self proclaimed Satanist. *Of COURSE that's why he had a goatee!*

He hoped the rest of the gang liked Anton as much as he did. He'd met Anton at a gig back in the city. Kevin had been floating from bar to bar, drunk as all hell and trying to find somewhere that sat right. He had heard the roaring heavy metal long before he even saw the small entrance to the club that was producing such a riotous din and the bouncer stopped him a clear six feet before he got to the door and shook his head, saying, *'Really don't think this is your scene, bro.'* But he offered no resistance when Kevin had shrugged and wandered past anyway.

His bones shook as he entered the venue which was all but empty. A few metalheads threw themselves around before the stage, as the lead singer, face painted white and streaked with black scars screeched about devils and blood into the mic.

It was a revelation!

All his life he'd never really known what to do with himself. People had expected him to fall into the same subcultures as his brother, but that held no appeal for him. He wasn't a *gangsta*. He wasn't much of anything. He still listened to rap, but it never spoke to him. Not like this, the raw and real emotion from the band whose name he could barely pronounce. He'd always thought of metal as a sideways step from the general geekdom he'd come to embrace by having Bilbo as a best friend, but he finally crossed that boundary the same fateful night he met Anton.

Kevin had been sitting at the bar, quietly drinking. The biggest of sore thumbs, sticking out. A black kid in a white hoody in a club full of white goths in black leather. Anton had approached him, naturally intrigued and struck up some light conversation. They had shared numbers and social media handles and began heading out to more gigs and within a month Kevin had found himself a new best friend. A month after that he had invited Anton out to middle of nowhere to join his annual camping trip.

They'd left Bilbo to his own devices and went exploring. Though Anton had shut down the use of the actual term *exploring,* saying it was childish. What they were doing was *manifesting destiny* instead. They trekked out, through the centre of the valley floor, crossing over the river via a scattered selection of rocks that made up its shallows and on towards the base of the mountain to their right, though neither of them knew if it was Alan or Allan. The trees converged back on them, swallowing them into the heavy woods once again and as they drew upon the cliff face proper they heard a voice.

Anton had turned to Kevin, holding a finger up to his lips as he dropped down to squat behind a tree, his leather pants squeaking, threatening to give them away. They crept forward, ducking from rock to bush.

The voice grew louder and then they saw the owner; Standing atop a boulder was a bald guy in a black tank top. His arms were as thick as the trees that surrounded them and he was practising karate moves. At first the pair were slightly awe struck, the stranger certainly looked the part but then they heard what he was saying. With each position he struck he'd call out the name of a *"chi power move"* that Kevin recognised from the popular Anime *"The Wyvern's Yarbles"*. He and Bilbo would watch it when they got high. Kevin quickly whispered this little fact to Anton and the pair had to stifle their laughter.

Huge dweeb or not, the wannabe action movie star was still likely to kick both of their asses if he caught them. Luckily, he had also set up a camera and was far too concerned with checking himself out in the reversed view-finder of the device to notice his spectators.

Anton gestured for them to retreat. They slipped away unnoticed and circled around the Seagal wannabe, finding his ludicrously decadent camping setup. He was riding a high end SUV with an extended flatbed that housed a veritable mountains worth of supplies. His tent was almost as big as Kevin's apartment and contained within was a portable television, stereo and gaming rig as well as a high-end hammock.

They crept through the camp, checking out the

ridiculous set up when Anton stopped, a mischievous grin plastered on his face as he explained his plan to Kevin...

They ran then. Sprinting back to familiar ground, following the overgrown pathways they had taken. Crossing through a clearing to throw off any attempt at tracing them.

'I still can't believe you just took it,' Kevin said, holding in a laugh.

'Do ast thou will, my man. It's like, the first rule,' Anton replied. 'Satanism 101'.

Anton held his stolen wares up. A bright red fuel canister, full and unopened.

'Why that though? Why not the Playstation?'

'He had five of these. I doubt he'll even notice.'

'Do ast thout will,' Kevin repeated. 'So cool.'

'So what should we do with it? I was thinking we burn a giant inverted cross into a field. See if we can find it on Google maps...'

A weird thought popped into Kevin's head after hearing the coolest guy he knew talking about committing grand arson with stolen fuel... just how well did he actually *know* Anton? He was *very cool* and fun and a big hit with the chicks. His real name was also Dustin. But was a Satanist really the kind of person to bring along on a camping trip? And why did Anton want to come anyway?

'Actually the Google satellite wouldn't be able to tell if the cross was inverted or not, would it? We'd be better off burning a pentagram instead.'

'Yeah,' Kevin said, his voice flattening somewhat. 'Can I ask you a question?'

'Shoot.'

'Why did you come along on this trip? I know we're best friends and all, but still... you'll be stuck out here in the woods with a bunch of people you don't even know. We go camping every year, but from the fact you're wearing leather pants I'm guessing you don't do this often.'

'Hey, I like meeting new people. I like doing new things. I've never camped before, but I've been to enough festivals to get the gist of it. Just drink enough so that you don't mind sleeping on the floor or shitting in the woods, y'know? Now how about letting me ask *you* something. You sure your friends are cool with me being here?'

'Yeah. Why?'

'Just don't want to intrude on your little club, y'know.'

Kevin laughed as they continued their homeward journey, 'We're not a club. We're just a bunch of people who like to hang out and-'

'Like the way a club hangs out?' Anton cut in.

'No. We just barely see each other these days. We were all real close. Real tight knit back in college. I guess everyone in the A/V class was. There was only *"Asshole Andy"* who didn't end up hanging out. Some people left though...' Kevin grinned as he prepared not to laugh when he said the next part. 'Jimmy quit. Jody got married...'

'FUCK YOU!' Anton cried out, his words echoing across the open ground, 'You do *NOT* quote that son of a bitch in my presence. I'd rather you read scripture than quote he who shall not be named.'

Kevin laughed even though he could tell Anton was genuinely a little bit pissed at him. Anton's triggers were all music related and Kevin already knew which buttons to press for a reaction. The biggest, reddest and most worn was the one labelled *"Bryan Adams"*.

'Are you bullshitting now just for an excuse to sing *"Summer"* at me?' He shuddered at the word.

'No.' Kevin said, before carrying on, 'I mean, yes? I mean... we were all a gang and people sometimes fall away, don't they? People *do* quit. People *do* get married and some people... I guess some people just move on. It's not like this is a screening process, but I bet when we leave here in a few days you'll have five new best friends. Well, we already chill with Bilbo a fair bit already... the math isn't important. The point is, come next year when we do this again we won't even have to think twice about you coming along, because you won't be an outsider next time. You'll just be an old friend.'

Kevin smiled and Anton followed suit. Kevin noticed it was a genuine one too, the one Anton had when he let his guard down where he showed off too much gum.

They walked on as the sun continued to dip and an echoing wail rang out across the valley. It was rich with fury and loss. Their faces dropped as they looked around at each other, then over their shoulder.

'Oh shit! He must have seen the missing fuel!' Kevin whispered.

Anton laughed and took off! Bounding into the tree line, back towards the camp.

The sun continued to slip away and darkness proceeded to take hold.

# 4.

'Lone survivor. Checking in. Log... 345. The time is... unimportant. Location... undisclosed. All you need to know is I'm seven clicks deep behind enemy lines and I have just one objective... survive!'

*"The Edge"*, as he liked to be called, gestured towards the camera hard with his thumbs as he finished his introduction, thinking how badass it looked. He'd finished his katas and had slipped into his ghillie suit. A heavy duty uniform and hood combo camouflaged with realistic looking moss, and leaves used to blend into the local flora. Now he was ready to start filming proper.

His spiel may have looked good under different circumstances. But the camera was framed wrong and had slipped a little after he had balanced it on a fallen tree. As it was now, the lens was only recording a pair of legs at a forty-five degree angle. He found if he had the viewfinder facing him he always ended up looking at himself, instead of the lens and that wouldn't do, not when he was shooting his first (and final) takes.

The Edge approached the camera and snatched it up, spinning it dramatically to face him as he began to stride through the woods, his voice drowning out the ambient noise; the sounds of his feet tramping through the fallen leaves and twigs, but also the faint footfalls of someone else too.

'Your number one objective when thrust into a survival situation is to survive!' he continued. 'To do this you need two things. Number one, water. Number two, food. And... number three. Your wits and cunning! In the following video series I will teach you how to do this... and more! You will bend nature to your will. You will break pain and fear over your knee. Using only what the land offers you and using only what you TAKE from the land... you will live... ON THE EDGE!'

The Edge had got caught up on his introduction and hadn't noticed exactly where he was going until he realised that, like a homing pigeon, he had instinctively walked right up to his SUV. The flatbed was full of water tanks, fuel and boxes of rations and cookies. All of which he'd just filmed, when he was meant to be out here with nothing.

'Aw FUCK!' he screamed. 'GOD DAMN IT! That was fucking perfect too! One take! Ruined.'

He snapped the viewfinder wing shut and stormed towards his truck. He opened the passenger side door and sat half in the truck. He reached behind him and into one of his many boxes of rations and grabbed a pack of Oreos and a bottle of chocolate milk. His rage subsided slightly as he devoured the cookies.

He smiled. He was going to be a star. Just as soon as he got all the footage required for the YouTube channel. There were so many fakes and phonies out there, filming guides and making mud huts in their mom's back yards. Not Dennis McDonnell though. Not *The Edge*. Because that's where he lived, and that's what he was going to show the world. He balanced on the very edge of what was acceptable, and he was the real deal... plus his mom died years ago. So her back yard was now his back yard. As was a considerable trust fund.

When the end came, be it nuclear war, viral outbreak, or via a horde of the undead, who was going to survive? He was. Him and anyone else who was smart enough and tough enough to learn how to survive out here.

The Edge hurled the chocolate milk bottle into the woods. He was here to live off the land, sure. But he would simply live off the land where he hadn't littered. There was enough of it, after all.

Picking up another pack of Oreos he leapt from the car, slamming the door behind him. He ducked into his large tent and picked up his brand new carbon bladed machete from besides the TV.

'Back to it!' he grunted.

He trekked out, far in the opposite direction of his camp and further up the ravine in order to make sure nothing of his gear could be seen when he started recording again. People would call him a fake if they saw his car. They'd be wrong though, he was the real deal, obviously. Though they had some nerve, after all he was making these videos for the normal people. They were the one who needed all the help they could get. He was generous like that.

He clambered up a steep slope, hoisting himself up the rocky outcrops using exposed roots from the trees as makeshift grips. His personal trainer had worked out an exercise plan and expensive dietary timetable that left him rippling with muscles, hence him being able to climb so easily. What was fake about that? He had the car and the supplies *just in case*. That was all. The tent and TV was so he could unwind after a hard days work.

Back on solid ground he unsheathed the machete and plunged it into the soil at his feet. He'd just thought of an even better, even more badass start to his video.

Once again he set up the camera and began. This time the device recorded a poorly blocked Edge approaching the machete which he pulled from the ground like an Arthurian knight claiming Excalibur. He jabbed the hefty blade towards the lens and began his introduction again as, over his shoulder, a figure draped in shadows, watched on.

After finishing, Dennis picked up the camera and without checking the footage, he closed the viewscreen and pushed on, deeper into the woods. This was his first time in a valley. He'd been on extreme camping adventures before, but they were always sanctioned and on monitored reserves. This was what he really wanted though. Something true. Something real. Something all natural.

He pulled out his Oreos.

The crackle of leaves and sticks had become an almost subconscious background noise, something the crinkling of the foil wrapping of the cookies broke with its entirely man-made and alien sound. He dropped the wrapper, finished off his snack and decided perhaps he should not stray *too* far from the truck as a nice chocolate milk and a few hours on Grand Theft Auto would really hit the spot.

The sound of him rampaging through nature continued, steady and even, matching his footfalls. Then came that foreign sound of foil again, as someone stepped on his discarded trash.

The Edge spun around, machete in hand, ready for

anything and there, brazen as day was his stalker. They didn't even try to hide themselves as the looming shadows of the under-brush did that job for them, obscuring their face.

He'd been training his entire life for this, hadn't he? What was he waiting for? He rose his machete up behind him and extended his free arm, an authoritative stance. He just hoped his stalker could see how hard he was flexing through the heavy ghillie suit.

'State your business!' He tried to say in a tone that matched his stance. But his voice came out two octaves higher than intended. He cursed himself under his breath and shifted, spreading his arms to his sides, holding the heavy blade out, perpendicular to his body. He hoped this display of strength and the *"come on then"* stance would compensate for the weakness he had just shown.

The gesture was met by the stalker shifting too, they flicked their arm quickly. Back, then forth. It was joined by a whistling noise, a dull *THUNK* and a sudden jolt of pain in the bicep of the arm holding the machete.

Dennis screamed. His voice ringing out across the valley. Any thought of the persona of *"The Edge"* vanished when the long, slender knife had struck him, sinking deep into his arm. Hot blood began to ooze from the wound as the limb began to spasm. He dropped the machete, which landed blade-first into the ground, once again waiting to be retrieved by someone it deemed worthy.

It wasn't going to be Dennis though. He took off, screaming as he went. He glanced back, glad to see he'd put some fair distance between himself and the assailant who was casually walking after him. All those hours on the treadmill had been good for-

There was another whistle and another *THUNK* as

agony shot up through his lower back. He staggered, tumbling to a squat, but did not fall. Running was no longer an option, so he turned to face his assailant and... nothing. The stalker had slipped into the foliage and vanished.

He stumbled backwards into the trunk of a tree, dislodging the blade in his back. The pain doubled and he howled as blood began to run down his buttocks and thighs. He tried to catch his breath and brought his free hand up to the knife lodged in his bicep. He knew he shouldn't remove the blade, but he wanted to be armed for when his attacker showed themselves again. It's what *"The Edge"* would have wanted.

He was still Dennis at heart though. He managed to yank the cold steel from his arm, but it reduced him to tears and his body began to go into shock. The knife slipped from his trembling fingers, and exhausted, he leant his head back against the tree.

Something flashed past his face.

In the split-second before his mind registered what it was, he thought it was another knife. Then his brain caught up and he realised it was a garrotte which promptly snapped tight around his throat.

Instantly he realised he didn't have enough air in his lungs as he tried, and failed, to draw breath. He whined through his nose as pressure began to build behind his eyes and the thick, gloved fingertips of his ghillie suit failed to find purchase on the taught strands of steel.

The pain vanished from both his back and his arm as he began to thrash, his whole body flailing frantically, trying to free itself. His face grew hot and turned blue. His eyes began to bulge from their sockets.

Flesh began to tear around his throat as he fought. The constant back and forth of his struggles were akin to a sawing motion, but he didn't register it, so great was his need for a lungful of air. Skin split, then his arteries followed as a waterfall of dull, oxygen deprived blood began to cascade from the freshly opened wound.

Still the garrotte held tight. Even when his kicks slowed and became post-mortem twitches. Only then did the stalker let Dennis drop.

As the body tumbled to the ground, the camera fell from the pocket that housed it. The view screen was cracked, but it was recording; switched on in the struggle.

It filmed the sunlight streaming through the leaves of the canopy above, then the light was obliterated as the shadow of the killer fell across the lens. They were backlit, indistinguishable, but perfectly framed. The figure contemplated the device for a moment before bringing a heel down upon it, smashing the equipment into the blood-slick ground.

# 5.

The sun nestled between the mountains as Donovan, Annie and Philly parked up besides Bilbo's Station Wagon and Kevin's out of place three door KIA.

Philly almost leapt out of the car, stretching and craning his neck after being cooped up for so long. His joints popped and clicked and it felt fantastic.

'What do we want to do first? Meet and greet or heavy hauling?' Donovan asked.

'I can smell Bilbo already,' Annie said. 'I'm going to say hello.'

She was right too. Philly sucked in a breath through his nose and where there should have been the fresh smell of the woods and grass and nature his senses were instead overwhelmed by the stink of marijuana. He had never understand the appeal of that stuff. He liked Bilbo, of course he did. EVERYONE liked Bilbo, but sometimes he wondered if the big guy's whole personality wasn't brought about by the weed he smoked. Regardless, he couldn't wait to see the big goon, Kevin too. The pair of them were the only other people he knew who could match him when it came to being giant geeks. He smiled.

God, it'll be good to see everyone again. Especially Zoe.

Instinctively he checked his phone. Still no signal, obviously. His message thread with her had ended with him receiving a smiley face. No kisses. That wasn't good. But still... after last year he was confident something would finally happen between them. They had wandered off together into the desert and lay beneath the stars and she'd nuzzled into his neck. She said she loved him, but then promptly fell asleep. The next day she couldn't recall anything, but the truth had leaked out in those drunken, dwindling hours and Philly just had to recreate that moment one more time and let it play out to its natural end.

'Yo! You coming?' Donovan said, throwing an arm around Philly's shoulder, nudging him towards the camping gear.

'Yeah. Let's do this,' he said.

From where they were parked they had to walk up a gentle slope to where the ground evened out and across the way they saw the fire burning and the huge shape of Bilbo sitting before it. He'd gained weight since last year. To his side was Kevin and... someone else. At first Philly presumed it was Zoe due to the long, black hair, but they drew closer and he saw it was a skinny goth.

'YOU'RE JUST IN TIME FOR BURGERS!' Bilbo called out as he used a long handled spatula to place the meat patties on the grill that stood over the campfire.

'What's up, guys? It's been too long!' Kevin said, meeting them half way. They embraced and walked back together, Kevin taking some of their bags. Annie almost squealed as she threw herself into Bilbo's gargantuan arms and he gave her a long squeeze. Donovan put his hand out, looking for a handshake, but instead Bilbo tugged him off balance and gave him a massive bear-hug too.

'And my little homie Philly!' Bilbo cried out, hefting himself out of his chair with no small exertion.

'Hey Bilbo,' Philly smiled as he was swallowed whole by Bilbo's embrace.

'We have GOT to talk about that new Skyrim DLC, my man. You played it yet? I set up a new Viking chick to play it and...'

Bilbo's voice trailed away as Philly caught the gaze of the new guy, the goth. Philly nodded and the stranger returned the gesture but who *was* he anyway? He wasn't part of the gang. He suddenly felt a little bit sick at the prospect of their dynamic being shook up.

With the introductions out of the way they began to arduous task of setting up their tents and gear around the fire. The smell of cooking food overpowered the spliffs which were being passed around and consumed along with copious amounts of booze. The gang were all chatting amongst themselves, Bilbo chewing Philly's ear off about his new character in his game, Kevin and Anton rambling to each other about music and Annie and Donovan just happy to sit there and take it all in.

Annie got up and sat on Donovan's lap, wrapping her arms around him. This was perfect, she thought. It was just missing Zoe, but then again it'd be weird if she was actually on time. She sometimes felt guilty about the way she felt when she was with her friends, but Annie felt more of a bond with the people around her than she did with her own siblings at times. Not that she didn't love Timmy-Boo and Kara, but growing up the three of them had had their ups and downs. Although it was mostly forgotten, and the ugliness their conflicts had wrought were brushed under the rug, the simple fact was that they were blood and she *had* to forgive and forget with them. The family she had here, on the other hand, were flawless. There was nothing she wouldn't do for her friends and likewise they would move heaven and Earth for her. They had all *chosen* each other and there was no slipping there. You'd never accidentally steal from your best friends and expect them to just forgive you, and that was the difference.

The sun vanished, the final rays peeking through the V-shaped valley receded, and the sky was replaced by the unpolluted and stunning view of the cosmos above.

Though for the small gang sitting in Death Head Valley, the world ended with them.

'I'm out. Damn, where do these things go? I swear I don't drink this fast when I'm not with you guys,' Kevin said, holding up an empty bottle,

'You brought more, right?' Donovan said. 'I've got spare, but don't drink them all.'

'Nah, it's cool. Got more in the trunk,' he said, getting to his feet. 'Anyone need anything while I'm down there?'

'Hey, I need some more chips,' Philly said, getting up too.

The pair set out into the relative darkness beyond the glow of the camp. Even when their eyes adjusted to the natural light of the stars and moon the surrounding woodland appeared to be a near impenetrable void.

'Watch any good TV lately?' Kevin asked as they made their way down to the cars.

He didn't need to ask though. They were both dying to talk in person about the thrilling twists and turns in the new season of the fantasy epic, *'The King and his Throne'*. The zombie dragons had finally risen from their graves, ready to do the bidding of the Lich Lord who, as it turned out, was actually King Billy's third uncle.

In the distance, within the darkness that made up the woods, a light flickered. Neither man saw it though, as they were so embroiled with their conversation. The lights blinked as it passed from tree to tree, gaining ground on them, and worse still, gaining speed. It wound its way towards them and then the lights were flicked off.

Kevin grabbed a pack of tall boys and Philly got his chips.

'What was that?' Philly said, hearing the roar of an engine, but unable to see its source.

'Shit, is that a-' Kevin began before the lights flashed back on again, blinding them as they froze in place, like literal deers in headlights. Kevin screamed, dropping his tallboys, one of them burst as it hit the rough ground and beer began spraying across the soil. Philly held up an arm, as if that might save him from the incoming, barrelling tonne of metal... but it was over almost as quickly as it began. The car came screeching to a halt, the brakes wailing out into the still night.

The car skidded, digging a trench into the soft earth with its rear tires and as the sound of the brakes pads faded and the engine died all they could hear was as tirade of swearing.

'Goddamn piece of shit car! Bastard shoe! Asshole!'

The main beams dipped out revealing Zoe's bug, painted yellow and adorned with hundreds of hand painted butterflies. Zoe's trademark and self proclaimed *"Spirit Animal."* The door opened and she pulled herself out of the car. Loose curls framing her pixieish face. She wore a heavy corduroy coat over a loose, butterfly patterned dress that stopped just before her giant army issue boots.

'Spare sandal got caught up in the accelerator pedal!' She exclaimed, a grin plastered on her face. 'I almost killed you both! Imagine!'

'And hello to you too, Zoe,' Kevin said shaking his head before throwing his arms around her.

'God, yeah. Sorry!' she cried out, her voice raising with excitement. 'Oh my God! How are you!'

Philly watched on, heart pumping as the pair finished their greetings. Then she turned to him, 'And you!' she exclaimed, wrapping her arms around his shoulders and planting a kiss on his cheek. He tried to turn his head to meet her lips with his own, but she was too fast, the kiss calculated and clinical.

'How have you been, Philly?' she beamed, taking his hands in hers.

'Great!' he said, then found himself just grinning like an idiot. He had a whole spiel planned out for when he saw her. A poetic and soul soaring collection of words and prose that would make he fall in love on the spot. But instead he let out a whining laugh and bared his clenched teeth. She placed a hand on his face and smiled. Philly's heart melted and, just as quickly, she turned away and marched up towards the camp. Like a puppy, Philly followed.

Zoe approached the campfire and screamed with delight as Annie leapt up and hugged her.

'Finally!' Annie called out. 'I knew you'd make it, but you had us on edge there!'

'I know, right? *And* I almost killed Philly and Kevin!'

'What?' Annie's face dropped, but Zoe was away and on to Donovan now, giving his butt a playful slap. She liked Annie and Don well enough, but they were a little *too* perfect for her tastes. They gave her a serious "Village of the Damned" vibe with their perfect hair and teeth. It was sometimes like they could read each other's minds. It was super creepy. It may have been jealousy talking though. She saw how Annie and Donovan bloomed so effortlessly, she wondered if they had ever been anything other than the butterflies that they were now. It seemed so easy for them, unlike Philly and Kevin who were, in her opinion, still gestating. She had tattoos, painted her car and had countless earrings depicting the beautiful creatures, only she knew she was faking it. She wasn't a butterfly, not even close. She felt she'd be a grub forever.

'Hey Zoe, been too long, girl. You want to hit this?' Bilbo said, grinning at her. 'You always say to save the trees, so this ones just for you.' He held up a fat spliff, making her forget about the slight blip that tarnished her otherwise stellar (if forced) self confidence.

'Oh my God! Bilbo you are the best,' she said, hugging him and sparking the joint, puffing away at it immediately. Now Bilbo was more her level. No pretensions there, no falsehoods. You got what you saw and what you saw was fun and a dude who was always holding the best weed.

Then she turned to Anton. He looked up at her from across the firepit, the flames wreathing his features and casting him in an orange glow. He smiled, his lips splitting only slightly, showing of a sliver of teeth. She felt the energy between them immediately. She swore blind to people that she could see auras. It was bullshit, obviously. Another ploy to show the world that she was the most intriguing of *Leidoptera*. She could feel vibes, but anyone with half a brain and half an understanding of human emotions could do that. Still, if people *did* have auras, she was certain theirs would have been going wild at the sight of each others.

'And you are?' she asked. They hadn't broken eye.

'Anton,' he said, taking a measured swig of his beer.

'I bet that jerk Kevin didn't even introduce you to everyone, did he? What a terrible host.'

'Hey, we don't need introductions. We just talk and get to know people that way,' Donovan protested.

'That's a load of bull and you know it, Donny.'

Kevin and Philly caught up with her and she turned and pointed at Kev who was suckling at the burst tallboy, 'You! You are an awful host.'

'Me? What did I do? I didn't do anything!' he cried out.

'Nothing! Exactly!' she turned back to Anton and gestured to herself. 'Anton, my new friend. This is Zoe. This is Bilbo. This is Philly, Donovan and Annie. How hard was that, Kevin?'

'Yeah, yeah. Queen Zoe does her thing. I get it,' Kevin smiled and sat back down next to Anton, passing him a beer.

'Well, with that out of the way. Are we ready to get twisted or what?' she called out, finishing her joint.

'Anton, could you?' Bilbo asked, gesturing to the portable Hi-Fi by his side. He was trying to reach it, but failing due to his bulk.

'Just hit play?' Anton asked.

Bilbo nodded and smiled. The button clicked and *"Bilbo's Patented Party Mix"* kicked in. He had the perfect ear for the music the group would all love, an eclectic mix of contemporary tunes along with a healthy dose of nostalgic tracks from their youth. Zoe squealed and began to dance, pulling Annie up with her because the first track was for her, *"Butterfly"* by Crazy Town.

Kevin turned to check Anton's reaction, knowing his Satanist friend would disapprove of the music, Crazy

Town had to be on his shitlist big time. But Anton was clearly enamoured with Zoe, beauty charming the wannabe savage beast. Though at the same time, sitting further into the darkness than the others Philly observed, watching Zoe glancing at the new guy who could not take his eyes from her. Philly's fingers had turned white with pressure as he tried, and failed, to crush the bottle in his hand.

'You have NO idea how good it is to finally hear some decent music!' Annie called out as they danced. The first few songs were always for the ladies.

'Don, you have those cheesy Eighties songs on again?' Kevin laughed.

'You have NO idea!' she repeated.

'Hey! Those tunes are called classics for a reason!' Donovan protested.

'Classics for grandpa's, maybe,' Bilbo said, to much laughter.

The hours passed as the drinking and smoking continued in full force. Eventually things began to wind down somewhat as Bilbo's mix took on a more chill vibe. Annie cuddled up with Donovan as Zoe sat besides Anton, her lavished attention fuelling Philly's exacerbated drinking. He was trying his damnedest to hide his spite, but Bilbo had picked up on it.

'This can't be your kind of music, can it?' Zoe said to her new friend. 'You have a dark blue aura. I can tell this isn't your kind of music.'

'So long as everyone's having fun. That's all that matters. That's one of the major teachings of the Church, even,' Anton said. Leading her to her next questions.

'The church!' she echoed, purring her words as she sat besides him. 'The church... of Satan. Sacrifice any virgins lately?' Her words were honeyed and oozed provocations.

Anton wasn't taken off guard though, after all this was why he'd gotten into the scene, wasn't it? Chicks loved the black sheep, bad boy act.

'I don't know any,' he smiled. 'Purity is so hard to come by these days.'

The group glanced at him sideways, not exactly sure how to reply to that. Kevin leapt to his friend's rescue.

'It's not so much a *church* though, right? More guidelines to live by.'

'I'm sure there's certain sects of Satanism and demon worship that go to black masses and offer blood sacrifices. I've read a few books about it and it's more popular than you'd think... but that's not what *our* kind of Satanism is about. At its core, the Satanism I follow is about realising that there is no God. That you, yourself, are God. Don't be held back by some dead doctrine from hundreds of years ago, you only judge yourself. So, for instance if you want something, you take it.'

He finished his spiel by turning to Zoe and flashing her another calculated grin which she returned.

'Is that why you stole the gasoline?' Philly spat. 'To appease the devil?'

Anton and Kevin's exploits had been a highlight of the evening. The kung-fu guy of the woods was set to be their most memorable character encounter. Perhaps moreso than the nudists they camped by a few years back.

'No. I took that because I'm an asshole,' he replied, getting a big laugh from Zoe.

'So cool,' Kevin said aloud by accident.

'Man, you should have lifted his Playstation,' Bilbo said. 'And the TV and generator to play it on.'

'He had a Playstation?' Zoe laughed. 'Tell me you're

kidding.'

'All true!' Kevin said. 'Makes you wonder why he even came out to the woods anyway. He basically had an apartment in the woods.'

'Sounds insane,' Donovan said. 'Though at least we know he isn't going to go all *Maniac Gardener* on us and hack us to death in our sleep.'

'Maniac *what?*' Zoe asked, laughing.

Annie leapt to her feet, shaking her head and hands.

'No! Don't get him started!'

Donovan turned to Philly and gave him a smack on the shoulder as he rolled his eyes. Philly shook his head in response, as if to say *chicks, man! They just don't get it.*

'Those cheesy horror movies?' Anton said.

'Horror *CLASSICS!*' Philly snapped.

'They don't make them liked they used to,' Donovan added.

Annie made her way over to the cooler and fished out more beers.

'What do you mean, *"don't make them like they used to"?* They're still making them! What are they up to now? Fifteen? They're *stupid* films. So, so... bewilderingly *stupid.*'

'She's only saying that because she's only seen part three... And she's an actual village simpleton from the olden days,' Donovan said as she sat back on his lap, passed him a beer and then punched his arm.

'So you thought this guy we stole gas from was a maniac gardener?' Anton asked.

'No, he might have just been a run of the mill maniac,' Donovan said,

'There's only ONE Maniac Gardener,' Philly stated.

'Wait, I remember those films,' Bilbo said. 'There were TWO gardeners.'

'Maniac Gardner 5: Topiary of Doom,' Philly said as

Annie caught Zoe's eye and the pair laughed, shaking their heads. 'One of his victims who survived went mad and tried to take over his mantle. Underrated, but I think it's one of the better ones.'

Donovan shifted forward and gestured with his beer filled hand, jabbing with an extended finger, splashing ale as he spoke.

'That's the beauty of Maniac Gardener! It's a simple premise and doesn't try to do anything weird or fancy! It's just a gardener who went insane and anyone who messes with his garden is doomed to a grizzly garden theme fate!'

'Lawnmowered,' Philly started.

'Hedge clippers to the face,' Donovan continued.

'Yeah. Cropsy style! Pitchforks as well, even if that's more a farm thing.'

'Trowelled.'

'Choked to death with the stems of a bouquet rammed down your throat!'

'Beaten to death with a gnome!'

'Classic. What about-'

'OH MY GOD! SHUT UP!' Annie cried out, smacking Donovan about the head. 'You nerds and those crappy movies! Why do I even like you?'

Bilbo began laughing and tried adding more kindling to the fire. He tried throwing it under the grille, but missed.

'Well that guy in the woods sounds like a maniac alright, but it also sounds like he'd die if he went more than three feet from a plug socket.'

'That's rich coming from you,' Kevin said, getting up and throwing the wood into the pit. 'I still find it crazy that we can get you get more than a block away from your X-Box and Lord of the Rings Blu-Rays,'

Bilbo nodded.

'That's true, that's true. In an ideal world I'd have a crib big enough for everyone to pile into. We'd all just chill and watch movies... marathon the Maniac Gardener collection as we get high as hell. But I live in a crummy, small squat. You all live on the four winds. So you know, when we do this little yearly getaway? Man... I'd sell all those Blu-Rays and game if I had to in order to hang with my friends and I don't care where it is or however many days I have to go without levelling my chick in Skyrim.'

'Bilbo!' Zoe cried. 'You huge dork. I love you!' She leapt up and flung her arms around him and the rest of the gang followed suit.

# 6.

Jimmy held the whiskey bottle up to his lips and sucked down the last of his Dutch courage. He glanced up at the mountain face of Allan and his head began to see-saw with a mixture of the booze and vertigo. He clamped his eyes shut, pulled in as much of the night air as he could and held it for ten.

It didn't help. Never did.

'Dang it,' he cursed and shook his face, hoping to wean out just enough of the alcohol that was tipping him over from useless to *truly useless*. But regardless of his state, there was no turning back now. His mind was set and he was going to do something. He wasn't going to sit idly by. Not today! How many years had that psychopath been killing people in those woods? He'd be damned if he'd sit back and let that tally go any higher.

He slung his shotgun over onto his shoulder and his feet passed from the pavement and onto the dark, earthen trail and entered the woods.

Traipsing around in the dark with a loaded gun and a belly full of liquor. He could almost hear Lesley now, saying he'd be more likely to kill himself through an accidental discharge than anything else.

*But better that than to die doing nothing at all,* is what he'd say back to her, if he could.

He shuddered. It was finally sinking in, how right that phantom trace of Lesley was. It would be so easy for him to die out here. These could be his final thoughts.

Despite the manhunt, the searches (which he'd taken part in) and the odd interferences from outside sources, they'd never found hide nor hair of Connor Finlayson, the madman of the valley. But he'd always believed. He knew that feral lunatic was out there, somewhere. He just had to keep his wits about him, make sure the bogeyman didn't get the drop on him.

*You could easily die out here!* he heard Lesley say again in the back of his mind.

He picked his way through the trees as the trail died at a dead end. Up ahead he heard the nameless river that came down from the flooded quarry. He'd follow it upstream to the more popular campsites. He hoped that's where the kids were anyway, so long as they didn't go as far as the quarry they might be alright. Story went that's where Connor made his home after the accident.

The river appeared to his left, the water sluiced past lazily. He stopped and splashed his face, the new moon reflecting off the clear waters, showing him his shadow self, features hidden by the black light... and there, besides him. Another shadow!

He yelped, dropping the shotgun into his waiting palm, spinning on his heels...

There was nothing there. What had he seen?

He rose his eyes to trees above him. A shirt, torn and faded was snagged on a branch that overhung the river. He looked back down at the water and it wafted over his shoulder. He'd mistaken it for a face, somehow.

'God damn it!' he snapped at himself. *You could easily die out here!* He'd be more careful next time.

He licked his lips and wished he'd brought more booze despite the state he was already in, but with the drink came memories. The legends of the missing kids. Not even teenagers like the rabble that drove through town. Children as young as seven or eight, plucked from their beds even as their night-lights promised them protection from the evils of the world.

He often thought of them, and his own children. They'd had four kids, himself and Lesley. He'd often wondered if any of them had survived, would that have been motivation for him to finally leave this godforsaken place? Though when Lesley died along with their fourth he had resigned himself to his fate here. He had also wondered about the heartbreak those other parents had felt, with their children stolen from them at age eight. Did it compare to his own pain when he lost his children before their actual birth days? He couldn't begin to imagine.

Then came tears. That'll be the gin, that.

'Could easily die out here,' he finally said out loud through huge, wet sobs.

And would that be so bad? How many nights had he sat in the garage with the same shotgun he held now, tucked up under his chin? Lesley was gone and with her were Marty, Tabitha, Johnny and John. It was bad enough that God himself was plucking away children so early, no way was he letting that bastard Connor take them away too!

He racked a shell, spat away the hurt and marched on.

The trees began to disperse along the riverbank and

his boots sank into the soft, loose soil. Each step harder than the last as he trudged on. He wasn't alone either. He could feel it. Eyes measuring him up, weighing their chances against him and the gun that bobbed, heavy in his hands. Not critters eyes either, not those of a boar or pig, human eyes.

The booze, exertion, and fear. It poured out of him as he screamed, 'WHERE ARE YOU? YOU SON OF A BITCH! YOU LEAVE THEM KIDS ALONE. HEAR? YOU WANT SOMEONE SO BAD YOU TAKE ME. YOU TAKE ME!'

That is what he wanted, after all. Right? Someone else to step in and pull the trigger after all those times he was too afraid to. Reunite him with Lesley and the kids. He wondered if they had been growing, up there in heaven. Marty would be a man himself now, if that were the case. Or were they still all babes, fresh from Lesley's belly. Asleep and waiting to be a proper family again before they'd cry out for the first time, waiting for their papa to sooth their fears of a life yet to be lived.

Tears again. Anguish and frustration.

'SHOW YOURSELF YOU DAMN COWARD!'

And speak of the devil... to his right, just behind the bushes, in the treeline. A shadow shifted slightly in moonlight that filtered down, shredded by leaves.

Jimmy turned and let loose with a snapshot.

The orange flash from the muzzle lit up the immediate area as the crack of gunfire ripped through the woods. In that brief moment when the pale, muted colours of the valley were replaced with a wink of orange daylight he could have sworn he saw the eyes of the beast itself.

The shadow was gone. The echoing gunfire faded, leaving behind the sound of rushing water behind him and his own rapid breath.

He pumped the grip of the shotgun, ejecting the empty shell and racking a new one. He eyes were still paper cuts in his weather beaten face. He scanned the trees and brought the gun to his shoulder, winking as he stared down the nub of the iron sight. It was a shotgun loaded with 12 gauge buck, after all. Aiming was really a cursory afterthought.

*This is it*, he thought, snapping his aim back and forth across the treeline. One way or another someone was about to die. He knew his own death would bring him peace, but what if he managed to take Connor down? Would saving the kids at the campsite offer him some sort of long-term respite? Would the nightmares stop then? Would-

A hand reached out from his blind side.

It snatched at the barrel of the gun and wrenched it upwards with terrible strength. Jimmy instinctively snapped his fist closed, causing the shotgun to let loose another riotous blast. Before he could do anything else, least of all try and pump another shell, the gun was ripped from his shaking hands and tossed into the river where it vanished with a heavy splash.

The same hand that had taken his weapon then socked him square on the chin, sending Jimmy spinning from the blow. The bastard was stronger and faster than he had imagined. How had he got the drop on him when he'd *just* seen him across the way? There was nothing he could in his dazed state to stop what happened next.

The same strong hand that knocked him down gripped his wrist, forcing it up his back. Then, as if he weighed nothing at all, the killer grabbed a handful of fabric at the scruff of his neck and hefted him towards the riverbed and forced his head into the coursing waters.

The freezing shock knocked him sober instantly and he let out a scream. His voice, carried by his precious expunged air, was washed away in the form of a stream of bubbles. He drove himself further into the cold earth as he fought the weight on his back, his mind racing. Some small part of it hoping Connor's bloodlust would be sated and hoping his sacrifice would mean the campers would be left alone.

By the same token, faced with his impending death he was certain Lesley and the kids could wait another few years before they saw him again. Surely if she was up there in Heaven with God, looking down, she'd do something to help keep his soul on this plane of existence for just a little while longer. *Surely?*

Even though there was none to be had under the cold waters of the unnamed river, Jimmy's body demanded air. His diaphragm contracted and instead of breath, his lungs drew water into them and the agony of oxygen deprivation was joined by the crippling pain of drowning. It was a terrible, but thankfully brief moment until his mind, starved of oxygen died and Jimmy was at peace.

Letting go of the husk in their hands, the killer placed a filthy boot against the sodden back of Jimmy's corpse.

They shoved it into the water, where it was swept away.

Whether Jimmy was finally with Lesley and their children was of little concern to his murderer as they sank back into the darkness. Their blood-lust far from sated.

# 7.

Morning passed without incident. Nobody stirred until at least eleven, the first of whom being Bilbo. He crawled from his tent with some effort, heaving himself back into his chair where upon he swore he would sleep sitting up that night. He lit a smoke, grabbed a donut for breakfast and began playing on his Gameboy.

Donovan and Annie were next, wearily getting to their feet, a hangover threatening to knock them right back down at any minute. The rest joined, all similarly worse for wear and Philly could not help but comment how the scene was like some small scale and real lame zombie uprising.

'Hope you're all ready for another day of fun and games, homies,' Bilbo called out, holding up some freshly rolled doobies.

'Maybe a beer. Hair of the dog,' Anton said.

'I might throw up,' Kevin replied, but all the same took a tin when offered.

'Which way did you say the river was?' Zoe asked. 'I need to freshen up.'

Philly stepped forward, about to offer to show her

the way when Anton spoke up.

'Hey, me too. Here, I'll show you.'

'A Satanist *AND* a gentleman,' Zoe smiled as they turned towards the creek. Philly couldn't help himself as a scowl crept across his face.

Bilbo watched on, recording everything that was happening and he could see Philly was hurting. Just as clearly he could see Donovan could not stop playing with the ring in his pocket, but Bilbo wasn't about to spoil *that* surprise. Instead he called out.

'Philly! Homie, c'mere.'

His face was ready to crack. It always had an air of tragedy about it, even when he was joking or gushing about a shared interest.

'Hey Bilbo.'

'Pull up a chair, man. We haven't had a proper heart to heart yet.'

Slipping his Gameboy away, Bilbo brought out his weed case, a little tub with various paraphernalia in it. He set about making more spliffs, grinding up the buds he had and constructing frames from the papers as he spoke.

'How have you been?'

'Fine, I guess. You?'

'You know me. I've just been chilling out, thinking. Chilling some more.'

'Sounds good. So how did you like the new episode of The King and his Thro-'

'Things not going so well between you and Zoe, huh?' Bilbo cut in, licking the length of the gum for his rolling paper.

'I guess not.'

'You know I was in love once, homie?' he said, sparking the spliff and offering it to Philly,

'I don't smoke. Thanks though.'

'I made it real weak. That's why I'm not smoking it. But here's the deal, I'm not opening my heart up to someone who isn't high, y'hear me?'

Philly looked at the *drug cigarette*, as he called them, and then at Bilbo who stared up at him with his half closed eyes. *What the hell!* he thought, accepting it and taking a drag, coughing hard as he did. He waited for a mocking laugh, but none came. Bilbo was cool, after all. Mockery was something that asshole Anton would do... probably.

'There we go. Like a pro!' Bilbo smiled, pulling out his own spliff which dwarfed Philly's. 'Now... where was I?'

'Love,' Philly said, his voice croaking. His head grew light.

'Mothafuckin' love! Her name was Cassie. She was beautiful and hilarious and every other dumb, vague thing you say about someone you love, because it's more than all that, isn't it? More than that, but you can't explain it, so you say that meaningless shit. More than their looks, how they eat, how they think... there's just an energy that feeds you when you're near them and it works the opposite when they're gone. It just fuckin' saps your life when they 'aint near. You get me?'

Perhaps it was the weed talking, but Philly was starting to think that maybe Bilbo was a genius.

'We used to spend near every day together. For months... years. That girl was something else altogether and I was a better man for being with her. You know the fucked up thing though, homie?'

'No, homi- I mean, no dude,' Philly gagged, then giggled.

Bilbo laughed too, shaking his head.

'The fucked up thing? She didn't love me back. Told

me straight after we hung the first month. Just one of those things, and isn't that just an asshole of a saying? *"Just one of those things."* But sometimes it is. You can't make someone love you, just like the way you can't *help* but love someone. Feel me?'

'But here's what you do. You tough it out for this weekend. Then you treat Zoe like she's a drug. It sounds like a horrible thing to say, and it is, my man. I don't take any pleasure in saying it. But I can't see you hurting, homie. You got to wean yourself off her, off that love, that energy she gives you. You gotta find that energy from somewhere else and if you're real lucky, you know where you'll find it?'

Philly shook his head.

'Like mothafuckin' E.T. said, man. It's right here,' Bilbo pointed to his chest.

Philly drew in another lungful of smoke and the pair stared at each other for a silent, reflective moment. He wasn't entirely convinced, but he sure felt a lot more relaxed after the weed.

'Thanks Bilbo,' he smiled.

'Lil' homie... you are more than welcome. Now tell me... who do you think is gonna take the King's throne? And what the HELL are they gonna do about that Lich lord and all those motherfuckin' dragons?'

Kevin joined them and the three of them delved into the deeper aspects of their favourite show. Things got a little heated however when the subject of the books came up. Bilbo, while loving the show, hated the author, calling him a *'Popcorn muncher's version of Tolkien'*. Philly knew just how bad the squabbling would get between Kevin and Bilbo and decided to take that opportunity to get himself another beer.

Donovan stood besides the cooler, staring down the incline to the car park where Annie was digging around for her water bottles in the back. He still could not remove his hand from his pocket, he flipped the ring over and over, fearing that with each pass his fingers would touch, the ring having blinked out of existence.

'Heading out?' Philly asked, cracking open the container at his feet and getting a beer.

'Yeah, we're heading out. Going to drive north, to the quarry. Have a look around. It's dug into the side of one of the mountain itself and from what I could tell from the maps we might get a good view from up there.'

In an ideal world he would have waited for another trip, somewhere with a nice hiking trail that would overlook the ocean as the sun dipped below the horizon, but he was too eager and excited and wanted to get the next stage of their lives together rolling as soon as possible. So it was either the quarry or they could try and scale the sheer faces of the Alan's without any hardcore mountaineering gear and break both their necks. He knew which option he preferred.

'A quarry in a valley up a mountain. Yeah, that sounds like a great time. Just you and Annie going?' Philly asked, though it was less a snarky question and more a thinly veiled plea.

Donovan could tell his friend was not having the best of times. Zoe getting familiar with the new guy was all he and Annie had spoke about the night previous in their sleeping bag. He didn't want to let his friend down though, but the proposal had to be a special moment, so he gestured for them to turn their backs on the car park and he pulled the ring from his pocket.

'Philly, I was trying to keep this secret, but...'

He flashed the band before tucking it back into his

pocket as quickly as possible.

'OH MY GOD-' Philly shouted, nearly tumbling backwards.

'Shhh! You'll spoil it,' Donovan said, reaching up, wanting to cover Philly's mouth.

'You're getting married!'

'Well, I'm proposing. If she says "yes" *then* we're getting married. But yeah. Obviously. I love her. This is my mom's ring too. I love her dude I-'

'Let me guess, you never stop thinking about her. She gives you an energy and she seems to sap it when you're apart. You can't even describe *why* you love her and other cliché crap which isn't so cliché when you *feel* it. Right?'

'Wow. Yeah. Well put.'

Where had *that* come from? Donovan wondered and how the hell could he explain it to Annie if he could not even get a single word of it out to Philly. He just hoped the ring would speak for itself.

'I just love her,' he said. 'I want to spend the rest of my life with her.'

'That's great, Don. She'll say yes, obviously. She's as crazy for you as you are her.'

'Thanks. But look, this is why we're going alone. I want it to be special. As special as proposing in a quarry can be, I guess.'

'It's unique! Might not be Paris in spring or Venice in winter or... I don't know, Botswana in fall... but you'll never forget it.'

'Forget what?' Annie asked and both Philly and Donovan flinched with shock.

'Your first quarry,' Philly said.

'Yeah. You never forget your first... quarry,' Donovan echoed, giving Philly the stink eye for his lame cover.

Luckily Annie was too busy digging around in her bag to hear them properly.

'I've seen a quarry before. It's just something to do really,' she said.

Donovan gave a sly wink and a thumbs up. Philly then mirrored the gesture.

'Are we going then?' she asked.

The SUV roared into life and they turned out of their glade and set off, following the trail to the far side of the valley, following the river that flowed down from the quarry.

Glittering beams of light refracted on the surface of the river from the late afternoon sun and Annie watched as fish leapt from the surging waters. She nudged Donovan and he stared over at the spectacle in silent awe. She rolled down her window and the roar of the river drowned out everything, even the truck's powerful engine.

The path grew steeper and diverted away from the river, leaving them adrift, lost in a sea of dense trees.

'Where would you build your perfect home?' Annie asked, scanning the woods, her answer already set in her mind. She'd resigned herself, and by extension, the pair of them, to renting somewhere in the city. It only just struck her how much she wanted something more for the pair of them.

'Anywhere so long as-' Donovan began before she cut him off with a smack to his arm.

'You say anywhere so long as it's with me and I'll puke and then kick your ass!'

'I wasn't going to say that!' he protested, rubbing his arm in mock pain.

'You absolutely were, you flake. Give me a real

answer. Where would you want to live?'

'If it's not where you want to live will you still love me?'

'Depends. Maybe. Is it a garbage dump?'

'It would be if you lived there with me.'

She hit him again, a little harder this time, but she kept her smile.

'The beach,' he conceded. 'A beach front house where I could sit in the sun all day, maybe go for a swim. Then listen to the crashing waves at night.'

'Ugh, you suck,' she said with a pout.

'No, actually, living on a beach is radical as all hell.'

'*"Radical?"* When did you turn into a surfer from the nineties?'

'Shut up,' he laughed. 'Go on then, where's better than the beach?'

'Here!' she said. 'Maybe not here exactly. But in the woods, or a forest, or whatever you want to call it. Out in the trees, somewhere beautiful... with a gorgeous view...'

Donovan's heart began to spasm as he pictured the view from the quarry top. Perhaps this wasn't about to blow up in his face after all.

Of course if the impossible happened and they *did* win the lottery and *could* live out this fantasy she would live wherever Donovan wanted, even in his tacky beach house. She'd be there in a heartbeat, because as much as she had chewed him out for saying he'd stay with her no matter what, the feeling was mutual. But that was her dream now, it was all so clear. A home amongst the trees. Just her, and Donovan and whatever family they chose to have.

'Weird,' he said. 'You know, in the woods was my second choice. It was just a slight fraction under my first choice.'

'You're pulling my leg!'

'Totally. But if that's where you'd want to live, then that's where I'd want to live too... so long as we're together.'

He turned and smirked. Annie returned the gesture with a smile of her own and this time she didn't hit him.

# 8.

Bird song filled the woods and it was just one small part of the symphonic background melody that accompanied the laughing duo as they raced through the cool shade of the forest across from the river.

Their joyous abandon drowned out the sounds the stalker made as he followed. He kicked past roots that were clogged around the base of trees and disturbed piles of rocks, but ultimately went unheard.

Zoe and Anton were too embroiled with themselves, too drunk on the sight of each other to see the shadow that trailed them. They staggered along the path, dancing almost. Arm in arm. Laughing about something their uninvited guest could not quite hear, and that upset him. What was this guy saying that made her laugh so much anyway? Perhaps it didn't matter. If someone finds you hot they'll laugh at anything you say... probably.

'Oh my God!' Zoe gasped, stopping suddenly.

The trees before them grew so dense as to form a natural wall. It curled around before them, creating a small cove. Above them the canopy was thick and intertwined, providing a cosy shelter. The floor here looked like a small pool, as bluebells had overrun the area and now they rippled in the gentle breeze, their faux waves undulating rhythmically.

'Would you look at that!' Anton said.

'I need to take pictures!'

Their stalker drew in, talking advantage of their distraction.

'What does something like that make you feel like doing? I don't mean, right now...' she bit her lip and met Anton's eyes. 'I mean, what does something like *that* make you want to do? In life?'

She took a few snaps before slipping the camera back into her bag and retook her position besides Anton. His hand hung besides hers for a moment before a force stronger than magnetism pulled them together, their fingers brushing before interlocking as they moved gently into the sea of bluebells.

'I'd love to say some feel good bullshit right now,' Anton said. 'Something about being inspired to paint or write or something... but I don't know.'

Just like their hands had moved of their own accord, the lovers turned to face one another. Zoe's spare hand slipped beneath Anton's shirt and all was silent for a minute. The bird calls, the critters, even the sound of the river seemed to fade away. It was the longest minute the stalker had experienced in his entire life. For the Zoe and Anton it felt like an eternity.

'You expecting a better answer?' Anton said with a sly smile.

Zoe bit her lip again and he leant in, meeting it with his own and they began to kiss deeply. His hands dropped to her hips and she cupped his face. He traced her panty-line along her outer thigh with the tips of his fingers then grabbed her ass, pulling her into him as their passion grew. Lips still locked they found their way to their knees,

Zoe pulling her skirt up, hiking a leg over Anton's waist who fell back, finally breaking their embrace. She straddled him, laughing before diving back down to resume their wild kissing amongst the flowers.

White hot fingers tried, and failed, to bury themselves into the trunk of the tree their owner was hiding behind.

Philly watched on. His paranoid fears given flesh as the woman he loved began to romp with a man he had only just met but hated more than even his worst childhood bully. He wanted to tear the tree from its roots, he wanted to crush Anton with it. He wanted to see him smeared across the valley floor.

Zoe straightened her back, crossing her arms at her waist and then with one pull her dress was lifted up and over her head revealing herself. Her hair fell back down around her face and Anton's hand instinctively rose and cupped her breasts, the left one emblazoned with a dazzling butterfly tattoo.

Their stalker forced himself to turn and run before their passions led them to their natural destination. He ran deep into the forest, away from the camp, away from Zoe, away from the heartache.

'God, that was great.' She said, pressing herself against Anton's still slick skin. His heart froze. What to say? Should he say anything? For the first time in a long time he wasn't sure where he stood. He settled on playing it cool and wormed an arm around the back of Zoe's head. She shifted to accommodate the limb and tilted her head to the side so their hair intermingled. They lay there amongst the bluebells, staring at the leafy canopy above and the thin trailing beams of sunlight that snuck into their private little world.

She fished around, blindly, for a cigarette. Neither of them wanting to break their unspoken skin on skin pact. Anton wondered if she meant what she said about their romp being *"great"*. The thought thrilled him. He just hoped he wasn't stepping on anybody's toes. He had only just met the rest of the gang, who knew what history they all had. But he *was* part of the gang now, right? It occurred to him that maybe his *"lone wolf goth"* thing was past due for retirement. He'd done his rounds with the chicks in the bars and festivals. Perhaps having some good, stable friends, or even a relationship, was what he really needed now.

'You want some?' Zoe asked, sparking her smoke.

'You know it,' he smiled, nudging his groin into her hip.

'Some of *this*, asshole,' she held the cigarette in front of him.

He pulled away from her, feeling the chill of the late day immediately after losing contact with her hot skin.

'Could I have that to go? I have to, ah...'

'What? Take a piss?' she laughed. 'Oh heavens to be! You'll burn my sensitive little ears if you actually said the word! Thank you for censoring yourself. Or I'd be confined to the pits of hell with your best friend Asmodeus if I were to hear a word of curse-'

'Alright, alright,' he grinned, taking the smoke and clamping it in his teeth as he slipped on his boxers and boots. He had always tried avoiding talking directly about bodily functions when he was with a new girl. Ridiculous, he knew, especially considering what they had just done. But the idea of them *knowing* he was pissing or... whatever, really irked him.

'I have to walk or my leg will cramp,' he lied, heading out into the brush.

'Well don't forget to piss while your at it!' she called after him.

He grinned. His genuine, disarmed smile, showing off way too much gum. He was just thankful she hadn't seen it.

Making his way around the walls of the small cove he came to a rocky embankment beyond. He scrambled down, trying to put some distance between himself and Zoe, lest she hear him pissing. He walked to the edge of the plateau he was on and the ground dropped away before him. It was only five feet, but the pattern repeated itself down the valley, like giants steps. There was nothing quite like the field of bluebells they had just made love in, but the bushes directly below him were blooming with vibrant yellow flowers. His anarchistic side decided this was where he should piss. Desecrating such beauty with his foul excretions was *extremely* Satanic. But as soon as he relaxed his bladder he felt a sudden twinge of regret.

'Too late now,' he said to himself as he listened to rhythmic beat of his piss on the leaves.

Zoe, the flower child that she is, would probably hate this. The *"Earth Mother"* or whatever she believed in would really hate it. Why *did* he have to be an asshole all the time anyway? Maybe he would make an effort when they got back to civilization. Especially if he hooked up with Zoe permanently. He could stop stealing, stop worshipping Satan, stop trying to look bad-ass when waiting for his bread to toast in the morning.

'Just got to be a better man,' he said. And he would, he decided. Right there and then. A wondrous future unfurled before his mind's eye. Him and Zoe renting a place together, they'd adopt a dog, take up painting together, get matching tattoos...

The sound of his piss hitting leaves was replaced by

the sound of liquid on tarp. The pattering, dappled thunder replaced by the sound of his stream hitting a solid surface.

What happened next took a mere few seconds to play out, but the horror unfolded much slower in Anton's mind, like in nightmares where the faster he tried to run the slower he went.

Below him, within the bushes, stood a person. His piss splashing against their shoulder. The figure was clad head to toe in black, waterproof fatigues, face covered with a similarly dark hood. The first ridiculous thought that flashed through his mind before the truth hit home was that it was Zoe standing below him, and maybe she was into kinky shit like golden showers.

Instinctively he tried to clench his kegel muscle to staunch his flow, but then he saw the knife and realised that pissing on someone was now the least of his worries. It was large, curved and heavy.

*Like the kind Rambo uses!* was the second ridiculous thought to flash through his mind as he saw the serrated back edge.

Shock kept him in place, trying to process how wrong this scenario was, and that's how the blade found him, legs locked, jaw slack and piss still flowing.

The shadow stabbed upwards, the knife slipping between Anton's legs and instantly his stream turned red as he let out a howl more bestial than human. His hands, still on his groin, gripped the area as tightly as they could as the shadow began to twist the blade and tugged him forward.

Suddenly the agony Anton felt was joined by the sensation of flying as he pitched forward, off the ledge. The trees spun around him until he landed on his back, in the foliage, his shaking limbs entangled in the branches of a bush. The yellow flowers within, now stained red.

The knife was brought up, over his stomach. The metal that wasn't stained with his blood gleamed. He tried to call out, to thrash and kick, but he was helpless as his limbs were entangled. The killer plunged the knife into his stomach, the heavy blade piercing him straight through.

Blood began to well from his belly, as well as pour out from his back as the killer stabbed him over and over, skewering him again and again. His body ravaged, the trickle that had started from the blood pouring from the wound in his crotch, soon became a deluge. It rushed out from under the bush, red and thick and trailed its way down the slopes, ready to be absorbed to nourish the flora that bloomed there.

Zoe stubbed out the cigarette amongst the flowers and immediately lit another. Her legs were still trembling and she wanted to be calm and back in control by the time Anton got back.

A cute, dark-horse Satanist. Now wasn't *that* something else. Of course she had him pegged (and *would* have him pegged, if she had her own way... and she would). He wasn't the real deal, just someone trying to get a rise out of society, but they were the best kind, weren't they? The angry and brash. Easy to rile up and bend to her own whims. Not in a cruel way, obviously, but she did enjoy the mind games that came with dating someone... O.K., maybe in a cruel way.

But they had to push back. There had to be some fight in them, otherwise what was the point? Anton? She could see herself pushing his buttons until they would nearly come to blows, get him good and riled before they'd end up ripping each other's clothes off and working out their frustrations wherever they fell. He had made a foolish mistake by admitting his hatred of Bryan Adams to her when they were sitting on the riverbank. That was a good one, she was sure she still had a CD of his back home too.

So long as he didn't change to try and placate her. If she wound up with *"Philly 2"* on her hands she'd be likely to top herself. That kid made her so mad at times. She was convinced she had been cursed to have every man in her life turn into a complete pussy.

Of course she hadn't helped. Getting drunk and admitting she loved him. She did, of course. Just not in the way he wanted her too. Perhaps something might have happened, if he didn't immediately become so dependant. But now he was more like a yapping pet dog she felt obligated to feed and dote on every now and then. His passive aggressive hints that they should date being the turds she had to scoop up with a newspaper every morning.

The cigarette burnt down between her lips as she dozed. She was picturing a new jewellery line for her online shop. A range *just* to annoy Anton with. Satanic iconography but with an ironic bent to it. A normal crucifix touted to be *"doubly inverted"* thus *"doubly blasphemous"*. A sigil of Baphomet but its runes would spell out *"LOVE"*. Maybe a-

A screech rang out. She sat bolt upright, it didn't sound human. She knew there were pigs somewhere in the valley, and that is what it had sounded like. The cigarette dropped from her lips and fell onto her breast, burning her just besides her tattoo. She answered the inhuman shriek with one of her own,

'SHITTY DEATH!' she hissed and licked her thumb, applying it to the singed flesh. She scrambled up, messily getting her clothes back on as her fingers shook from the fright.

She slipped on her boots, and called out.

'Anton? You there? Anton?'

His clothes were still bundled besides the indentations they had left within the bluebells. She considered picking them up before heading out to look for him, but figured the clearing would be easy enough to find again. She followed Anton's trail, the leaves and twigs haphazardly snapped and bent where he'd trampled them. She followed him down the steep, natural steps that had been carved into the earth.

It was quiet. She hadn't noticed before, what with their laughter and talking and... other noises. What had happened to the birds and creatures that serenaded them so sweetly before? Besides the distant river, she was the only one making noise and that frightened the hell out of her. She could not help but feel like any loud noise on her part would alert some kind of predator, deep within the woods. She saw it speeding towards her, roaring as it came, bounding over fallen trees and dodging rocks until at the last moment she'd turn around, too late, and the evil force would barrel into her.

'Get a grip!' she spat. Too many Evil Dead movies, she figured. 'You're smarter than this.'

Though her sense of hearing felt like it had been cranked down, her sense of smell was still being overloaded by the scents the woods brought: The fresh sap, the earthy thickness that came with fresh soil and... the strong, acidic reek of ammonia? She pulled a face. She was close now, Anton was probably trying to pull some dumb prank. She braced herself for him to jump out at her, and sure enough as she scanned the trees that surrounded her, she checked her rear and there he was. A few meters away, hiding behind a tree dressed head to toe in black.

'I see you, asshole,' she called out with a smirk. 'This another one of your silly little *"Satan"* games?"

Purposefully, she marched towards him and caught another smell. To her right, something was lurking in the bushes and the stench was strong and all too familiar. It was Anton. His face, turned upside down from where he lay on his back, gazed up at her with cold, open eyes as blood soaked into the earth beneath him. She recognised that odour now, how could she have ever forgotten it? His body was red and slick, dark, gaping cavities dotted his burst abdomen. Zoe screamed.

The figure behind the tree, whoever it was, stepped out and extended an arm. In it was a long boar hunting spear. The tip was winged, ideal for causing maximum damage and would prevent the unlucky victim impaled on it from freeing themselves. The shadow gripped it with both hands and began to advance.

She quelled her voice and ran! She swung to her left, back towards the camp. She'd rally the troops and get out of there, then call the cops. She was smarter than to try and let them tackle this by themselves. They'd be back; with cops and helicopters and guns. She rushed through the woods, clambering the slopes and darting between the trees and over rocks, much like the speeding force she had imagined chasing her before. Roots threatened to snag her feet, branches tried to clothesline her, anything to let the lunatic at her back catch up, but she was not about to let that happen. No matter how thick and fast the obstacles came at her, so long as she kept herself aware she'd...

She passed a spear. However it was not in the hands of a killer. It was driven into the ground at a forty-five degree angle, its deadly tip aimed upwards and outwards.

Realisation hit her all too late. The killer had lined a proximity of spears on the path back towards the camp, counting on her running full bore into the field of traps they had set. And like clockwork she did just that. She could not stop, and her momentum ran her into another spearhead.

What little breath she had was knocked from her as the cruel implement punched through her belly, driving straight through her abdomen, and bursting out of her back between her lower ribs.

Her mouth filled with blood which sluiced out over her lips, soaking her chin as she retched and coughed. Her legs bucked slightly and she slipped further down onto the makeshift stake, tearing her guts even further. She gripped the spear, trying to pull herself off it, but the pain and the slick shaft prevented her from managing to move more than an inch.

She heard feet casually approach from behind. *'Why?'* she tried to say, but the word was garbled and just brought more blood pouring from between her now red teeth. She wanted to see her killer, to see the monster who had brought such a cruel end to her life before she had fully bloomed and emerged from her chrysalis. She wanted to look them in the eye, then spit in it.

The killer did not grant her that satisfaction though. Instead she felt something strike her hard between the shoulder blades. The spear pushing through her, crossing by the one that had punctured her guts. The second spear passed through her and deep into the soil below.

Unable to slide down either shaft now she let go of the spike as the last of her life left her body. And there she died, pinned to the earth like a sample butterfly on a lepidopterists display board.

# 9.

Annie and Donovan reached the quarry later than expected, the valley was deceptively larger than what the maps had led them to believe. They had driven up a steep and winding path which criss-crossed the river via wooden bridges that appeared to be on the verge of collapse. They had left the valley floor behind long ago and to their right, every so often, they caught a glimpse of the staggering drop that was lined by the canopy of trees below. It was an impressive sight, but Donovan knew there were better to be had.

The path evened out finally and led to a clearing where the woods had been decimated. Stumps and ancient, felled trees littered the ground. The quarry workers would have cut them down long ago. Lumber littered the ground, unused and rotten. It was still swollen and bloated from the rains that had swept the valley a few days ago. Folks in the town proper had worked the quarry, but the trek out was arduous and in its heyday the place was a popular destination for those seeking work, so more housing had to be built, and why not build it in the valley itself? Donovan had seen the shanty town on

Google maps, it was on the far side of the quarry. They decided they would gather the rest of the gang tomorrow, maybe, and go exploring.

To their left a waterfall thundered into a large lake. It cascaded down the sheer mountain face of Alan (or was it Allan?) through a large, jagged crack that looked like a child's representation of lightning. They gazed up at the ragged cliff face, mottled with green where nature had found root in its unforgiving and brutal nooks and crannies. It was the outer side of the quarry. Perhaps, given time, the workers would have expanded and the entire cliff side they stood on would have been a large, gaping wound into the side of the mountain.

'Looks like we're walking,' Annie said.

Leading up to the top of the quarries outer rim was a trail that led through a natural canyon of sorts. A steep path nestled between the rock and had been lain with wood and gravel. They left the SUV and followed it up, through a ragged pass and onto the flat plateau above. Once they were level they could see the yawning hole that had been blasted into the side of the mountain, then down into the earth. Normally quarries are miles long with gradually dropping paths for trucks and excavators, but this one had steep, ringed paths that led down to boarded over orifices just above the waterline. They could see now that the river originally ran *around* the quarry. The old guy in town had said there had been an accident, but it looked like the ground between the water and the man-made fissure had been intentionally blown away to flood the place. However, nature always found a way and the quarry maintained a relatively even depth as the excess poured out of the crack they had seen.

They approached the edge and peered over the lip and into the dark, sightless depths of the pool below. The water was clear, yet the sunlight barely pierced further than a few feet before being extinguished by the depths.

'What were they mining?' Annie asked.

'No idea. And why *didn't* they just mine it out? Why a quarry?'

Neither of them were geologists though, all they had was baseless speculation and the quarry was not the real reason they were there anyway. Donovan turned around and looked back, over the valley. THAT was why they were here.

He called for Annie to join him at the edge of the plateau. She made her way over to him, stepping over the large cracks and jagged edges that made up the floor.

'It's beautiful,' she said.

A sea of trees stretched out before them, the river snaking into them and disappearing from sight. The green vista reached out across the valley, and they could just about see the plains they had driven across on the horizon. She gazed up at the mountains, the atmosphere misted, their peaks faded in the distance of the lower atmosphere.

Donovan couldn't take his eyes off her face. Her expression as she took in the view was magical. She caught him staring.

'What are you doing? That's weird. You're weird.'

'But that's why you love me,' he smiled.

'Sure. And you're super handsome.'

The ring was hot against his skin. Slick too from his nervous touch. His stomach wanted to purge itself, but there was nothing to expel. He had skipped breakfast for that reason specifically. He pulled the band out and kept it tight in his fist as he turned to face Annie front on, she followed his lead, wanting to embrace in front of the natural beauty of the valley. They kissed knowing they would remember this moment for the rest of their lives.

'Annie...' he said, their lips parting. The taste of her working like a sedative, calming his nerves and stopping the shake in his legs. He took to one knee.

'Oh my god,' she whispered.

He reached into his fist with his spare hand and held up the plain ring. He had a whole spiel about it being simple, just like the love he felt for her. Simple and easy, natural, the way it was supposed to be. But the words didn't come, nor did they need to.

'Yes!' she cried out, wrapping her arms around him as they kissed again.

He slipped the ring onto her finger and she held her hand out. It was loose. He had never bought a ring before, never even thought about them. He especially never thought about resizing them, nor did he think about the fact his mother had been a burly, thick woman. And, as Annie moved her hand, the ring fell from her finger and bounced off the stone floor, towards the quarry mouth.

A howl of panic ripped from Annie's throat as she raced after the ring, Donovan following in hot pursuit.

It struck the ground, letting out a high pitched ring, then again with each consecutive bounce, putting more distance between it and its pursuers with each strike. Its momentum slowed and, just before the looming chasm where it would be lost forever in the dark waters below, it skittered and began to roll, before slipping into a crack in the rocky floor.

Annie cried again, all but throwing herself across the coarse ground and reaching into the dark crevice to fish out the lost jewellery.

'Watch you fingers!' Donovan called out.

'It's alright. There's...'

Her voice trailed off as she pulled out a large, faded pin badge. She held onto it and plunged her other hand back into the hole, retrieving the precious ring which she then slipped snugly onto her thumb.

'Thank God,' Donovan said. 'That's my mom's.'

'I'll keep it on here until we get home. Then we can get it fitted properly. I love you,' She said as they hugged. Then added, 'Your moms? Oh my God, Don... I can't believe it.'

'It's not too corny, is it?'

She didn't respond, instead throwing herself into him once again.

'What else did you find?' he asked when they finally pulled away from one another.

She held up the badge. It was almost as big as her palm and was decorated with cartoon balloons and presents. The colour was all but gone and the metal that held the plastic coating in place was solid brown with rust. She rubbed a finger across the muck encrusted surface and read the message out loud, 'Connor. *"Eight"* today.'

'Some kid lost his birthday badge up here, huh?'

'Yeah,' she replied quietly. 'A long time ago.'

The drunk from town had mentioned a Connor, hadn't he? He saw his family die and grew up in the valley, feral, taking his revenge on anyone who came near.

She shuddered, even in the warmth of the afternoon sun.

'You ok?' Donovan asked. 'You've gone pale.'

She didn't know what to say. She didn't want to sully the proposal and Donovan would think she was mad for believing the ramblings of the town drunk. After all, the badge was at least twenty years old, if not more. How could a child have survived out here that long? If there was any truth to that story, (and there had to be, she held the proof there in her hand) then the resolution was one of a tragic loss of life. A child's family, then the kid himself, dying of exposure or hunger. It wasn't the origins of some campfire bogeyman. Even so, she felt unwell thinking about it.

'We should head back,' she said, unable to hide her fear.

Try as she might, she couldn't hide the fact she was terrified from Donovan, and every five minutes he would ask if it was the proposal that had knocked her sick. The car was cruising back down the path and she found herself staring at the trees that whipped by with a new sense of dread. They didn't fight much, usually when drunk and over petty things, but she could feel a fire building inside her, mixing with the dread and fuelled by the wrongness that badge had brought about in her world view.

Donovan drew breath and Annie's fingers pulled up into fists, she was ready to scream, but instead he swore.

'SHIT!'

His leg began pumping the brake pedal, but the car didn't slow.

'The brakes!' he cried out.

The SUV continued to roll down the gentle decline before thumping into the low point of a dip, hopping over it and coming to a sudden, jolting stop as they bumped into a tree. It was barely a fender bender.

'Jesus Christ!' Annie said, hopping out of the car.

Donovan followed and fell to the floor, checking under the car.

'Brake lines have snapped.'

Annie felt that dread inside her well again, she felt

like throwing up.

'Don, we have to get out of here!'

'Not going anywhere with the brakes shot. There's some way steeper paths than this one. Unless you want to slowly cruise down, pumping the handbrake, but that'd fuck it-'

'Who cut them, Don?' she asked, pleading. How could he be so calm?

'Cut them? Nobody. Probably got snagged on a sharp rock or... why would someone cut them?'

'Connor,' she finally admitted. 'Don't you remember the old guy in town?'

'I thought his name was Jimbo or something.'

'No! Don! He said there was a crazy guy in the woods called Connor. He cut our brakes!'

'Hey now... hey,.' Donovan cooed, wrapping his arms around the trembling Annie. 'Crazy old guy was drunk as hell. Just trying to scare us for shits and giggles. God knows there's nothing else for them to do around here.

'And look,' he continued, 'if it was this *"Connor"* the *"mad man of the woods"*. Would he know how to cut a brake line? And if he did, then what was he expecting? He's been watching too many movies if he was expecting us to blow up or something. They always keep their foot on the gas in films, you just let off the accelerator and let the car come to a stop. Y'know, unless you live in San Francisco on those crazy steep roads. Worse case scenario we would have been banged up a bit.'

'Banged up a bit? And that's fine, is it?' she yelped. He started strong with putting her at ease but fumbled the ball at the end.

'I didn't say that, Annie...' he held her out at arms length, and stared into her watering eyes. 'It was a creepy coincidence, I swear. That's all. Nobody out here but us and that idiot survivalist. But you heard how he was set up, just some dumb kid playing in the woods. We'll hike back down to camp, get Bilbo to fish out a repair kit and tomorrow he can drive us back out here and we'll go home early, if that's what you want? Ok?'

She nodded, but could not shake the terrible feeling something was wrong... and in his heart of hearts, Donovan felt the same way.

# 10.

Night had come. The stars lit the tree tops, but not the spaces between them, and no-one had returned to camp. Kevin paced the perimeter with a warm, untouched beer clamped in his hand.

'You're making me dizzy,' Bilbo said, blanket tucked up under his chin.

'You're not sleeping out here tonight, right?' Kev asked.

'Sure. Why not?'

'You'll freeze! You've got a nice tent there and an inflatable mattress.'

'No, it's good. It's good. I'm comfy, there's enough fuel for the fire.' He unhooked an arm from his coccoon and shook the stolen gas can. 'It's good. I'm going to smoke under the stars.'

Kevin approached and sat down with him, putting the beer aside and grabbing a new one. It was not easy to forget about five missing people, even when talking to the big guy who had the ability to wrap you up in his little world.

'I have a theory that dreaming under the stars will

make your dreams richer,' Bilbo said with a nod, widening his eyes to get his point across.

'Guess there'll only be one way to find out. But seriously, dude, don't try putting that gas on the fire. Just stick to the wood.'

'I know, man. I was just joking.'

Bilbo reached forward with his extended spatula and placed a burger on the grill over the fire and nodded for more kindling, which Kevin added. The flames leapt as the fat sluiced from the meat and landed amongst the embers.

Kevin turned and glanced back out into the void that surrounded them, unable to shake the dread that had wrapped itself tight around his spine.

'Can't get lost here,' Bilbo said, trying to ease his friend's troubled mind. 'They'll all be back when they're back. Can't get lost here, not really. The valley is wide, sure, but you just have to look up at the mountains to tell if you're getting deeper into it. Annie and Donny are probably screwin' man. Want to get it out their system before they get back to camp. Don't want us hearing them.'

'I guess.'

'Same with your friend and Zoe.'

Kevin grunted.

'You cool with that?' Bilbo asked. 'You're not jealous or anything? I knew Philly had a thing for Zoe. That lil' homie just needs some space.'

'No, I'm not jealous. Zoe isn't my type,' Kevin said. It was true as well. He'd never admit to it, but he *was* slightly jealous but not of Anton hooking up with Zoe though. The thing was... Anton was *his* friend. He missed him and was slightly perturbed by the idea Anton might forget about him altogether if things got serious.

'Chicks dig that goth look, huh?' Bilbo said, balancing his burger on his long spatula, trying to flip it onto a bun. 'You going to start painting your face white?'

'You telling me to white myself up? Not cool, dude,' Kevin smiled, playing Bilbo's game.

'I meant like a Dracula goth, asshole.'

'I know. And no, I'm not going to dress like a Dracula.'

Bilbo finished his burger and lit another joint, passing it to Kevin who had a toke.

'So what's with you and Anton, man?' Bilbo asked.

'What do you mean?'

'You two are getting real close. Just didn't know you were so into that heavy metal shit.'

'It's just different, I guess... you know, you grow up and people expect certain things for *your* life *for* you. Know what I mean? Like my brother, Thomas. He calls himself *"Tommy-Gun"* now. Thinking he's part of that whole gangster rap scene. Like he's from Compton or The Bronx or some shit. I've never seen a real *"Gangster"* in my life.'

'What do you mean, you're talking to one right now!' Bilbo grinned.

Kevin laughed and carried on.

'I mean, I love it, the music and all that. It's great and I get it, but it's not *my* life. Not mine and Tommy's lives. I've held one gun in my life and that was at a rifle range at some dumb life-camp thing our parents sent us to. I don't *"pop caps"*. I don't *"pimp"* and I only occasionally smoke *"dank kush."*'

'Nothing wrong with some kush now.'

'I'm not saying it's a bad thing.'

'I think I get it, man,' Bilbo said, blowing a huge plume of smoke out of his nose. 'This world is an ice cream parlour. There's a thousand different flavours and combination of flavours, and if you're real lucky sometimes it's an *"all you can eat"* kinda day. But you feel your Tommy is limiting himself to only having Rocky Road with walnuts and you feel people expect you to do the same. But you want some of the real weird Ben & Jerry shit, like fish flavour or something.'

Kevin laughed again.

'Sure! Something like that. Sure. What about you? What flavour you after?'

'Man, I don't give a shit so long as it has sprinkles, sherbet and strawberry syrup,' Bilbo said, his head almost bisecting as he grinned.

'I tell you what is good-' Kevin began, but stopped when he heard something. Over the crackling of the fire he heard a distant popping that barely reached his ears. 'You hear that?' he asked.

Bilbo shook his head.

He got to his feet, stumbling slightly, not used to the potent weed Bilbo smoked and stepped away from the campfire. He strained himself, listening for the odd noise again and-

There it was. And it clicked as to why it sounded so familiar. It was the sound of distant, breaking glass. He turned to the *"car park"* and heard another pop, then a brief flash with an adjoining "whoop" as an alarm started and was just as quickly silenced.

It was the karate survivalist!

It had to be! He'd found them and was wrecking their cars as revenge for Anton stealing his gas!

Another pop. Another busted window.

He paced back and forth for a moment, trying to collect his thoughts. Bilbo was of no use. He loved the guy, but unless he could be rolled down the hill like the fat kid in *"Hook"* he'd be useless in a fight. Ideally he wanted Donovan here. That guy was built and took, and gave, beatings like no other, thanks to his football days.

Bilbo was dozing, head nestled into his giant shoulder. Kevin began to panic, horrible ideas of this 'roided out survivalist killing his friends over some stupid prank crept into his brain.

*Oh God, no. Is that why nobody has come back?* he thought and took off, down towards the cars.

He could talk it out with the guy. Sure he could... or take a beating like a man and hopefully not get murdered.

The warm glow of the camp left his back and the chill of the night crept in as he navigated his way down to the car park under the starlight, the washed out colour of the land was dotted with impenetrable shadows and his mind played tricks on him making them appear to undulate and breath rhythmically. He heard more broken glass, much louder and much closer this time.

He passed by Bilbo's station wagon and the windows and tires were fine. He thanked God. Maybe he had just misheard and-

A crunching shuffle caused him to snap around. He was not alone. The dude was here, the military man, and his mind went back to how big the guy was and all the karate he was doing. Sure, he had laughed at the dork for screaming about anime, but the guy looked like he could rip a tree in half if he wanted to. Kevin looked from car to car, bush to bush, he couldn't tell where he was. His camouflage gear was hiding him perfectly.

'H-Hey?' Kevin said, as loudly as his breaking voice would let him. 'I'm really sorry about the gas. It wasn't me. I mean... it was, but I'm sorry. It was a stupid prank. It's at the camp. You can have it back! We haven't touched it, I can buy you more. Please...'

Anton's car had been smashed up. Payback enough in his mind. Then he noticed that Zoe's bug had been wailed on too, her back two windows having been put through.

'Shit, sorry Zoe,' he said, then, to the darkness. 'Hate me, blame me! It's my fault, not my friends. Leave their shit alone.'

He leapt as Zoe's bug lit up, letting out a familiar *"Whoop"* as the alarm was tested. He span around and in the middle of all the parked cars stood a figure who held the FOB for Zoe's car. They clicked it and the car fell silent again. They wore all black and a hood that covered their face. It did not look like military gear, but perhaps the survivalist guy had some weird spec-ops clothing too? The stranger then drew their other arm from behind their back, in their fist they held a small club.

'I'm sorry,' Kevin repeated. 'Did you hear what I said about the gas? It's untouched, it's-'

The stranger stepped forward and in a flash they brought their bat across Kevin's face, sending him reeling. His cheek bone shattered, teeth were knocked loose and the sky began to spin, the stars became a gigantic kaleidoscope. He still tried to plead his case though, but all that came out was a mumbled mess of wet, smacking sounds.

Kevin raised his hand, to try and defend himself, or to try and show submission. Whatever would stop what was about to come next. In response the stranger raised their own arm, club and all. Then brought it down, smashing into Kevin's hand, shattering every bone within it, wrenching his fingers backwards. Kevin howled through the agony of his broken face and the stranger hit him again over the back of his head.

The stars began to spin faster as Kevin pulled himself into a ball to protect himself from the beating. He felt as though he was seeing double now as his brain was rattled around in his skull. Through his swollen eyes he felt like he was seeing two shadows raining blows upon him. He felt his ribs give, his left knee was cracked and as a blow crushed his lower back his bladder gave way. Then... respite. The attack stopped for a brief, wondrous second and the blazing aching of his injuries were heaven compared to the blossoming agony of fresh blows.

A hand went to his neck and gripped his shirt and his attacker began to drag him towards Zoe's bug. Through the brain-fog, and the thundering sound of his own rapid pulse, he heard the lock snap open and weary creak of a door opening.

Next came the feel of cold metal on his throat as the killer placed his head inside the car door, hooking his chin over the lip of the frame and letting his body hang limp. Kevin began to choke slightly, unable to move his busted arms, but it didn't last long. With and almighty kick, the killer slammed the car door against the back of Kevin's neck, breaking it.

They kicked again and again, each blow ravaging the now dead man's neck, ripping into it with each consecutive impact. On the eighth kick the door slammed shut. Kevin's body flopped to the ground, sans head, which rolled into the foot-well of the bug.

The alarm began to sound.

The gloved hand of the killer clicked Zoe's FOB and shut it off once and for all.

Bilbo knew people who didn't dream when they smoked weed. They claimed it was some chemical thing.

They said that because the weed was effecting the neurons of your brain that deals with dreams all day, that when you actually fell asleep the brain just did not know what to do with itself... or something along those lines, he wasn't a scientist.

He was just glad to be the exception, because Bilbo had some weird dreams.

The cusp of reality was just on fading from his focus. Kevin had vanished into the night, leaving just the camp, the fire, and the stars. Bilbo was no longer wrapped up in a blanket, but magnificent wizard robes like Gandalf the Grey and the fire at his feet was the diabolical Balrog he had to battle through the underworld, only it was claymation like that old, crazy kids show from England, *"Trapdoor"*. He'd be damned if he would question it, because the whole ordeal was radical as all hell.

Elements from the real world would seep in every now and then. The cry of someone far off, the whoop of an alarm. The Balrog was a master of deception as well as a master of karate, after all. But Bilbo ignored its deceptive attempts to try and stop him from defeating it and bringing back peace to Middle Earth.

'Psst,' the Balrog hissed, its giant, rubbery mouth rippling from one side to the other. Claymation worms wriggled out from between its teeth as they appeared and vanished beneath a wave of plasticine.

'Psst!' the worms said, each one louder than the last.

'Psst!'

'PSST!'

**'*PSST!***

Bilbo woke with a start. His blanket had slipped and lay besides the fire. He kicked it up with his feet and wrapped it around himself again then rubbed what little sleep had accumulated away from his eyes. Had Kevin gone to bed? Had the others come back? He checked his watch. It was near enough midnight. Ideally the party should have just started.

'Psst!' a voice whispered from behind him. He flinched with shock. It was a remnant from his dream. It had to be. He craned his neck and saw nothing but darkness.

'Kevin, my man, that you?' he asked, but the darkness didn't reply.

He shrugged and began making another spliff.

It was probably Kevin trying to play a joke, or Anton, drunk and rowdy trying to impress Zoe. He was not going to fall for those games. So long as he had something to smoke, something to munch on, and his imagination he wouldn't need to move one damn inch.

He leant over, got some wood and added it to the already large pile of ash and cinders amongst the dying embers of the fire. Then he threw in some paraffin cubes to get it going again properly. He should also throw another few burgers on now that he was awake again. Maybe some s'mores.

'Psst,' the voice hissed again. He couldn't tell if it was male or female either, could have been Annie, for all he knew. But that was not her style and he wondered how the proposal went and whether to act dumb when they told him about it.

With the fire roaring again the heat began prickling his bare legs where the blanket didn't reach. He got his long spatula and places a s'more on it, a pre-bought one. But he decided he would only pop it on the grill for just a second. Let the chocolate get gooey. He grinned at the prospect.

A sharp pain jabbed him in the butt.

He let out a yowl and sat forward, trying to grasp the area where he had been pricked, but his bulbous frame was preventing him from accomplishing the task.

'What are you doing, man?' he asked the prankster. Waking him up and making noises was one thing, jabbing his ass with whatever it was? That was beyond the pale!

It still hurt. He could feel his shorts becoming damp too. Whoever it was had drawn blood.

'Psst,' they said again, finally getting a reaction from Bilbo. With some level of exertion he hauled himself out of his chair and stumbled on slightly on numb legs. He was already out of breath and slowly turned around and saw blood on his expensive, high tensile chair surrounding a tiny gash. He shook his head, he was not an angry man, but this was beyond anything he'd have ever expected from his friends. He landed on the only possible suspect, Anton. He was new and clearly did not know the line. Stabbing him in the ass was one thing, but the chair? The tensile strength required to keep the thick fabric together must have been immense, a small tear in it like that could compromise it altogether.

He stepped around the seat, towards the wall of nothing that seemed to surround the camp. He peered into the void, swearing he could see someone out there, a shadow a shade lighter than the natural blackness it inhabited, but perhaps not.

'Hey man!' he called out. 'Not cool. I mean that seriously. You seem chill to me, Anton, but we're not that kind of crew, you hear me? We don't do *"pranks"* and if we did we wouldn't be stabbing no asses.'

Bilbo stood there for a minute or two before he stepped backwards, keeping his eye on the shadows, hoping Anton would come forward, be a man and apologise. But he never did. Bilbo picked up his blanket and found one end of it was ragged, cut to shreds with a knife.

He fell into his chair, staring at his wrecked sheets, now furious beyond belief.

'MOTHERFUC-' he went to roar, as he saw the gift that had been left on the grill.

The red jerry can lay on its side, top open with the shorn off length of his blanket stuffed into its open neck. Flames raced their way up the fabric, towards the hungry, volatile gasoline kept within.

Bilbo opened his mouth to scream. There was a flash of light. Then nothing.

# 11.

Donovan turned off his flashlight as they found a path that opened into familiar ground. The moon had risen high enough to illuminate their way clearly now and, although it was unlikely the flashlight would run out of juice, Donovan was relieved as he had not brought any spare batteries.

They heard a distant cracking as rocks came loose and fell from their resting place, slipping down the mountain and barrelling into trees. It exemplified just how silent the valley had become.

'How much further?' Donovan asked, his arm slung around Annie's shoulder for warmth and comfort. The lack of any bogeyman leaping out at them over the past few hours had settled their nerves a fair bit.

'I'd say ten minutes. Depending on the lay of the land we might be able to see the fire soon.'

'God! Something real to eat,' Donovan groaned with pleasure. 'I hope Bilbo hasn't finished all the burgers.'

'That'd be great. I just want to cram some food down me and fall asleep.'

It had been a long hike, they'd eaten their cracker

rations and were starting to feel the first pangs of hunger. She thought of the warm double sleeping bag too and the air mattress they had. She hoped it didn't make too much noise either. They wanted to consummate their big news. What would she say to the gang tomorrow? How to even broach the subject without sounding like she was showing off? Who else knew?

'Don?' she said, ready to quiz him, she had a feeling Philly was privy to his proposal plans. 'Who else knows ab-'

The valley was filled with light for a brief moment. Warm, orange flames lit up the far mountain wall where their camp was and brought colour back to the plants in the surrounding area for a second, followed by the sound of the explosion. A resounding and deep eruption of noise, bouncing from mountain to mountain. The sound faded, but was replaced by the thunderous rumble of another rockslide.

'HOLY SHIT!' Donovan cried out, pushing Annie down, covering her with himself.

'OH MY GOD!'

Luckily, like with the brake lines, it was Donovan's turn to have taken lessons from movies to heart. They were way out of the blast radius and clear of any debris that rained down. When they thought it was safe again they looked out, across the field at the dying flames. However something drew their attention away from it; walking towards them was a human-shaped shadow.

The moon did not refract any light from the figure's dark clothes and it gave the figure the optical illusion of appearing to be cut out of reality itself. A hollow, human shaped void with eyes for them.

The pair stared at the advancing shadow, dumbstruck for a moment before Donovan spoke.

'We should run. Shit! We should run!'

He pulled on Annie's arm, and they ran! Bounding away down the path in order to circle around towards the camp. Annie glanced back to see the figure following them, stepping up its casual pace to a mild jog. They were in good shape, they'd outrun their pursuer easily... she hoped.

The rhythmic sound of their feet hitting the path filled their ears as they followed it around towards the impromptu car park. Confusion swept across them; the cars were all wrecked. Tires slashed, windows smashed in, and the hoods were all open, battery wires yanked out and frayed. Surely if *anything* was going to have caused the explosion it would have been one of the cars.

They passed by the shell of Zoe's bug and caught sight of the remnants of Kevin that lay, decapitated, besides it. He lay in a thick pool of blood that appeared black in the moonlight. Annie shrieked and Donovan tried, and failed, to contain his own caterwauling.

'What the fuck? What the fuck!' Donovan began to say, over and over.

Annie turned away, tears blurring her vision, and not six feet away from them stood the shadow. The person who *had* to be the killer. Whoever it was held their arms behind their back and appeared to have been casually waiting for them to catch on that they were there. How had they got here so fast? How hadn't Annie or Donovan heard them? They had put so much distance between themselves and the bastard, it didn't make sense.

Donovan rubbed away the tears that had streaked his face.

'Run!' he shouted. Annie was not sure if he meant her or the killer.

He pulled his jacket off and gripped the heavy

flashlight like a club and took a step towards the shadow.

'I don't know what you've got behind your back there, but I'm going to shove it up your fuckin' ass!' he snarled.

In response, the killer revealed the gun they held and without any pantomime they levelled it at Donovan and pulled the trigger. The action was joined by a flash, the crack of the bullet leaving the barrel, and Donovan spinning where he stood, blood spraying from his back.

His body pirouetted, twisting around itself as it fell besides Kevin's remains. Annie stared at him in shock and before Donovan's eyes closed he managed to spit out one final, repeated word.

'RUN!'

Gunshots rang in her ears as she ran up the hillock towards the camp, the earth either side of her erupting, spraying sodden clumps up into the air as the bullets slammed into the ground. She shrieked as she propelled herself forward on all fours, unable to process what had just happened. She just knew she had to find someone! Anyone! She'd be fine, just so long as she found someone...

The ground levelled off and she raced towards the ruined remains of the camp. The tents lay strewn across the ground, shredded and wrecked where debris and shrapnel had tore through them along with the coolers and hampers. She was surrounded by remnants of flames that slowly burnt on, fuelled by whatever scraps they had landed on after the explosion.

Worst of all, amongst the carnage, lay the body of Bilbo.

She retched and brought her hand to her mouth as she saw what was left of him. A dead, unblinking eye gazed off into the darkness. There was a crater where his second eye should have been, shards of his skull were exposed along with scraps of twisted metal. The burns raced down the entire right hand side of his body from where he had turned, trying desperately to avoid the explosive contents of the jerry can. His body was tore asunder, the flesh flash-cooked as it was pummelled by the shockwave, splitting his large gut. A loop of still sizzling guts was splayed out on the ground before him.

Annie heaved, though nothing came up. She wanted to collapse. The shock, her friends, Donovan... she wanted to collapse right there and let whatever may come just happen and be over with. Though instead, the world spun and her body, rebelling against her soul, was running through the woods and thankfully, no more shots came.

Much like Zoe before her, she ran through the trees, avoiding the treacherous hazards that littered the woods. She ducked beneath the branches, leapt rocks and avoided looping vines that threatened to snatch her neck into a natural noose. Though unlike Zoe, Annie would not be caught by the treacherous traps of the killer. She had skirted the area where Zoe and Anton had been slain, but she did not avoid discovering what had become of Philly...

A slick mess had been left covering the ground before a large oak and, as Annie raced pass, she slipped and fell, sprawling on her hands and knees. She stood up, shaking, checking her palms. They were slathered with a mixture of blood and muddy soil. Then she saw the remains.

A large tent pole speared Philly to the tree at his back, he hung a clear two feet from the floor. He was missing a leg and an arm. Each limb appeared to have been wrenched off with a horrific amount of force. The skin where arm met shoulder, and leg met torso, was a ragged trail of gristle and flesh. The removed extremities lay beneath the body, not missing at all, though she wished they were when she saw what had happened to them. Fresh, red wounds were dotted along both arm and leg. Bite marks. Human sized chunks of Philly's flesh had been ripped from the bone by some cannibalistic lunatic.

She wailed and looked up at his face. His expression conveyed a sense of pain and horror Annie could not even begin to understand. His eyes bulged from their sockets, his lips hung slack and she knew her poor little friend had been alive throughout most of what agony had been wrought upon him.

'Philly...' she bawled and tried to run again, but her legs had turned to jelly and she had lost all bearings of where she was. The trees had swallowed the sky and in turn, the mountains too. She heard the distant rush of water and staggered in its direction, hoping to find the river and following it downstream, and hoping to find a way out of the valley.

It felt like an eternity, but only minutes had passed when Annie came across someone hunched by the river. It was a portly woman rinsing her hands. She wore slacks and a plaid shirt, but Annie recognised her regardless. It was the waitress from the diner. Annie stumbled towards her and the woman finally saw her.

'My God...' she said, shocked and taken aback at being caught wet handed.

'Please...' was all Annie could get out, her body began to shake uncontrollably, the adrenaline leaving her system. 'Please help.'

'There there, sugar,' the woman cooed, wiping her hands on her shirt. 'You're alright now, Maisie's here for you.'

She wrapped her big arms around Annie who fell into the woman's embrace and let her head fall upon her shoulder. Maisie continued to whisper calming words into her ear and Annie felt like a babe who was being held for the first time. She felt her eyelids grow heavy, but something felt wrong, her brain had already made the connection and was waiting for her body to catch up. On the riverbank, there was a shadow that was much darker than those surrounding it. It took a second or two to parse what she was seeing, but it was a bundle of clothes. Heavy duty, black clothes.

Annie pulled back, staring at the bullish face of Maisie who was smiling now. A genuine, content grin and completely alien to the forced, sad grimace she had put on the first time they had seen her. But there was no way this woman the one responsible for the deaths of her friends. How did she end up here if-

'All in hand, Maisie?' a voice asked from behind her.

Annie turned to see a man in a Sheriff's uniform. Under one arm were bundled his own black clothes. His other hand lay upon a holster at his hip, containing within the pistol that had taken Donovan's life.

'No problems here, Sheriff Montrose. Right, honey?' Maisie asked, tightening her grip around Annie, turning her around and throwing an arm around the young girl's throat.

'NO! NO! NO!' Annie began to scream as she kicked and thrashed, trying to wriggle free from her captor. Montrose remained calm and undid the latch that held his gun in place, but Annie didn't care. She wanted to reach up and dig her thumbs into his eyes. She wanted to rip his throat out with her teeth. He would have to empty every bullet he had into her chest to stop her. He...

Her thoughts grew clouded, pressure began to well in her ears as Maisie's choke-hold grew stronger, cutting off the blood to her brain. The world span again, as it had done so many times that night, but finally it brought with it darkness and some morbid kind of peace.

# 12.

'Wake up.'

A hard shake accompanied the voice that slipped into Annie's fogged mind. She couldn't piece together what was happening at first. Had she been drinking? What was the bad thing that happened? And why was that voice so familiar? She tried to open her eyes and her head spun. It felt like she could hear the liquid in her brain coursing around behind her eyes.

'We're not carrying you. Get up.'

She knew who it was now. The bastard who shot Donovan. The darkness behind her eyes was replaced by the speckled void of stars in the night sky as she fought her way back into consciousness. Agony followed, the cold cramping feeling of laying on freezing soil. She tried to push herself up, but her hands were bound before her with rope and she promptly fell back to the ground, face first. A laugh went up behind her, followed by a wolf whistle.

'Cut the shit, Francis,' The Sheriff said.

'Or what Montrose?' came the second voice. It was dirty and thick. It was the pervert from their stop at the diner.

'You'll cut the shit or I'll see to it that we drain you first when we get up top.'

Annie craned her head around, instantly recognising where she was. The rushing water was a familiar waterfall, whilst all around her lay stumps and fallen trees and lumber. Surrounding her stood Montrose, Maisie, Francis, and an old man she did not recognise. They had put their dark robes back on and had their hoods up. Francis was ogling her ass.

Montrose stepped up and leant down, hooking a hand under her armpit.

'He's the least of your worries,' he hauled her to her feet, pulling her close. 'You've been doing well up to now. Better than your friends, anyway. Keep your mouth shut and don't try anything cute and this'll be quick and painless. None of us want to drag you up the path there, especially old Arthur, but try anything or say anything and I *will* break both your legs and your jaw. Understand?'

She turned to meet the old man's face who nodded and spoke.

'Better do as he says, honey.'

'Up to you,' Montrose said and gently pushed her towards the steep path up to the quarry. She staggered forward, knees threatening to buckle beneath her. Maisie led the way. The clearing was full of cars and trucks and Annie realised the whole town had been in on this from the beginning. Her and her friends had never stood a chance.

Moonlight lit the quarry-side, causing the grey slate floor to almost glow in the natural gloom. The moon, however, held no dominion over the quarry pit, leaving it a yawning black abyss.

Before the darkness stood its children, another twenty acolytes, all dressed in black robes. They turned as Annie was led across towards them, Montrose strode ahead, raising his arms.

'Tonight's the night!' he called out. 'I'm sure you can feel it as much as I can. *They're here.* Tonight we embrace immortality!'

'What is he talking about?' Annie whispered, mostly to herself. Maisie leant in to reply, but the cultists who were gathered before the pit parted, revealing a shirtless figure who had been forced to his knees, bound as she was. She almost collapsed in shock.

'DONOVAN!' she cried out.

He tried to right himself, to straighten his back, but it was too much. She saw the bullet wound in his upper chest had been sloppily cauterised. It was swollen and oozed pus. He was under the thrall of a terrible infection. He stared at her with bleary eyes and smiled, mouthing something before the effort took the wind from his sails and his head fell forward again.

Hands gripped Annie's shoulders as they drew closer and she was forced to her knees across from her fiancée. An acolyte stepped forward and passed Montrose something pale and cylindrical. He held it in both hands and stared at it, his eyes growing wide with wonder.

'How's the boy?' he asked, not looking up.

'Not doing too well?' a guy with a thick moustache answered.

'He's not about to die any time soon, is he?'

'Infection'll get him in a few hours, I'd say.'

'Good,' Montrose stepped forward and placed the item he held between Annie and Donovan.

She was drawn to it, though she wished not to be, as its visage caused an intense primal revulsion within her. It was white, and veins ran through it like marble. Upon its surface a relief had been carved, a demonic face with absurdly deformed features. Its mouth was twisted across the left hand side of its face, thick lips parting to show rows upon rows of tiny teeth. A thin, flat nose sat above the mouth and either side of that were two black orbs. They were darker than the abyss of the quarry behind it and if it was not for the wet sheen that caught the light and made them look alive, Annie would have have believed they were bottomless pits.

'Is it time?' the old man, Arthur, asked. His skin was so thin Annie could trace the blood vessels beneath it. He was on edge and shifted from leg to leg.

Montrose looked up at the stars.

'Not yet.'

'I could drop dead any second! Get on with it!'

Annie began to cry, the tears finally materialising. They'd been threatening to come since she woke up.

'Why are you doing this to us?' she blubbered.

'You wouldn't understand,' Maisie said.

'You're not from the valley,' Montrose added. 'You never had the dreams. Never heard the call. Never heard *them*. We have neighbours here. You can't see them or feel them, but we can hear them. It's like listening in to a conversation in the next room by putting a glass to the wall. And let me tell you, the walls here in the valley are real thin.'

She baulked. Her body was trying to cope with the lunacy and failing miserably. Her friends were dead, the love of her life was dying. And because of what? Lunatic devil worshippers in the woods?

'Why though?' she repeated, knowing full well she would never get an answer that could justify what they'd done.

'Why?' Montrose said. 'Immortality. We offer a sacrifice of blood and death. The death of your friends and their blood, and then we offer a vessel for our neighbours. That way they can commune with us. And then, as a reward, we'll be granted eternal life.'

'Soon I hope!' Arthur yelped. 'I'm old as shit and about to fuckin' die! Get on with it!'

'You're not going to die, Arthur. Shut up,' Montrose snapped.

'Fuck you!' Annie spat. 'You killed my friends to make-pretend that you'll live forever. Fuck you! Kevin and Bilbo and... oh God! Philly! You bastards *ate* him. You ate parts of him while he was still alive. You sick bastards.'

Montrose furrowed his brow and looked around at his fellow zealots, confused. Then, in turn, they began to cast accusatory glances amongst themselves.

'Ate?' Montrose asked. 'Who? Which one was Philly? Who killed this *"Philly"*?'

The congregation shook their collective shoulders, mumbling their innocence about the suggested cannibalism. They raised their voices, claiming it was against the rules. Against what they had been told. The blood was sacred and for spilling only. Never to be consumed.

'That was the weird skinny kid, wasn't it?' Maisie asked.

'Yeah. Not seen hide nor hair of him,' Francis added.

'You might be suffering from a bit of stress there, miss,' Montrose said to Annie. 'We're not cannibals. That's not our M.O.'

She lowered her head and forced her eyes closed. She felt her nails digging into the palms of her hands, wishing they were driving into that son of a bitches eyes instead. She blinked and saw the cracks in the ground and remembered the badge she found.

'Connor!' she gasped. 'It was Connor!'

It made sense. She had wondered how he could have survived. He'd be a wild beast, wouldn't he? Hunting and eating anything he could get his hands on. There were still lost tribes in the Amazon who practised cannibalism. Its taboo was a social construct, after all. It *had* to be Connor.

Montrose laughed as the acolytes snickered.

'Connor Finlayson? The wild boy of the woods?'

'He's real. He's out there!' she said.

'Starting to sound like old Jimmy there,' Maisie said. 'He never heard the call. Too many bad dreams of his kids, I think.'

'Connor was a real person,' Montrose continued. 'But he's long dead. He was one of the first kids we tried to use as a proxy for our neighbours... nothing came of it though. We didn't have the process figured out and now he's down there-' Montrose pointed behind him, to the quarry's pit, '-With your friends.'

Besides him, framed by the darkness, Arthur was staring up at the sky. He blindly reached out for Montrose's arm and yanked it.

'Stars are right! Do it now!'

Montrose nodded and pulled a small, curved blade from his robes. Annie tried to kick herself up, but multiple hands gripped her shoulders and pushed her back down. Instead she began to scream as Montrose leant in and without a word, drew the sacrificial knife across Donovan's throat.

Almost thankfully, in his addled state he barely seemed to notice. He coughed once and after a seconds delay a torrent of blood began to cascade from the grievous wound, soaking his chest and pooling around him. Annie continued to scream as the blood began to make its way towards the hideous totem before them and vanish. The notion that the statue was absorbing the blood was ridiculous. It was trickling through a crack beneath the thing. It had to be. The idea that Donovan's blood, his essence, was being drank repulsed her to the core. He twitched, kicking as the deluge at his neck slowed and finally stopped. Then he crashed forward. Dead.

'Well?' Arthur snapped.

'Well what?' Montrose said.

'Where are they?' Francis asked, Arthur's nervousness rubbing off on him.

'It can take a while. You know that.'

Annie watched as the last of Donovan's blood vanished into the stone. Her tear ducts had ran dry. She felt cold and calm. She was next on the chopping block, she knew it. But she would go down fighting. She demanded vengeance and given the opportunity she would kill every last bastard there, though she'd settle for just Montrose. He held the knife. He pulled the trigger. He was in charge here. She would make him suffer before she'd let him die.

'It's not working!' Arthur cried out.

'You can feel them! I know you can! We all can!' Montrose protested.

'Might be the girl they want,' Maisie said.

'O.K. then,' Montrose nodded to two of the acolytes and they stepped forward, seizing Donovan's body. They hauled him to the lip of the quarry's pit and tossed him over the edge. The world went quiet for a moment and then came the echoing splash of Donovan joining the countless others within the pool below. Another secret to be forgotten in those dark, consuming depths.

Arthur turned back from the darkness at his back as he spoke.

'Open her up. Let them in.'

Montrose vanished behind Annie and brought the blade to her throat. She tried to fight back, but the arms held her fast. *Donovan was gone.* She thought, feeling the fight leave her. Not just dead, but *gone.* Lost, just like she would be, and all of their friends, and somehow that was worse. Their bodies would never be found. Their parents and loved ones would never know what happened to them. Knowing their demises, no matter how horrific, would have given their family some kind of closure, at least.

'What if it doesn't work?' Francis asked.

'It will. It has to. We'll make them manifest tonight. Somehow,' Montrose said. Annie read between his words. He would be willing to drain every last member of the cult in an attempt to summon the *neighbours* he spoke of if he had to.

Annie looked into the face of the idol. Then past it, past where old Arthur stood on the cusp of the quarry's pit. She saw a hand reach up, over the lip of the abyss and her heart leapt. For the briefest of moments she thought it was Donovan. He'd survived, somehow, and was back with blood on his breath and vengeance boiling in his veins.

Unfortunately she was right on all points bar the hand belonging to Donovan.

It was heavy set and encrusted with filth, the fingernails were black with grime. It brought with it a heavily muscled arm which was covered by ragged clothing that was too tight and had burst in several places.

Then the figure's head came into view.

He wore a grubby white cloth wrapped tightly around his face leaving a mop of short and unkempt hair hanging over the edges. Two holes had been ripped out of the canvas for eyes, but the shadows rendered them as dark pits which reflected only the slightest glimmer of moisture from within. Below the holes, daubed with blood, were two lines that twisted around the side of his face as a mockery of lips.

Annie's eyes flicked down to the idol, then back at the intruder and realised the mask was a tribute to the dark deity portrayed within the stone before her.

Someone saw their new, uninvited guest and screamed.

Then things devolved into utter madness.

# 13.

The figure rose up behind Arthur, dwarfing the old man who cried out weakly as he was scooped off his feet and effortlessly held above the masked man's head. He was suspended for a moment, before being brought down across his extended knee. Arthur was broken in half, the back of his head near enough meeting his own ass as the sickening echo of his breaking back cracked across the quarry.

Behind Annie, Montrose dropped his knife and went for his pistol. The figure cast Arthur's broken body aside, flinging him nonchalantly into the pit.

Gunshots blasted above Annie's head, deafening her. Blossoming red wounds erupted on the killer's broad chest and he staggered slightly before falling flat on his back, just shy of the drop.

The zealots drew back in after their initial, panicked retreat. Annie's hearing came back and she heard them yammering on, quizzing each other about the stranger's identity. Annie knew who it was though. The legends were true. He'd survived when they had tried to use his body for their arcane magiks, and he had survived in the valley all this time.

Maisie approached the fallen killer, a heavy hunting knife with faint remnants of blood on it in her hand. Francis followed, holding onto a boar hunting spear.

With all eyes on the body of Connor; Annie reached forward for the knife Montrose had dropped. She slipped it between her knees, blade up and began slowly working on her bonds.

'Get that mask offa him. Let's see who the hell it is,' Francis said.

'Hold on a minute,' Maisie said, leaning in, knife held out as if she knew the killer was about to strike. Which is exactly what he did. She lashed out with her weapon, but Connor was much faster and snatched at her forearm with a hand that encompassed it easily. Reacting entirely on instinct, Francis thrust his spear forward, straight into Maisie's back as Connor yanked her sidewards, using her to shield the blow. She wailed as Connor pulled the hunting knife from her weakening grip and jabbed it forward, skewering Franco's throat. Connor released his grip, leaving it there, flush against the perverts Adam's apple. Francis let out a shrill, wheezing howl as both he and Maise fell down. Dead.

Some of the braver acolytes rushed in, knives and clubs drawn. They set about Connor, opening him up, spilling his blood, but if he felt the pain from the attacks he was not showing it. He reeled from the force of the blows, but as soon as he lay his hands on someone they were dispatched with a ferocious efficiency. He drove his forehead into their faces, causing their noses and eyes to erupt, speckling his mask with gore. He wrung necks and lashed bodies over into the quarry where the faint sound of them striking the cold waters barely broke through the cacophony of screams and yells of the melee.

Behind her, Annie heard Montrose swearing to himself and then the pattering of feet as he turned tail and fled. The ropes around her wrists were sufficiently worn, so with a surge of energy she ripped her hands apart, freeing herself. She snatched up the knife and followed Montrose, leaving Connor to his slaughter.

The wails of agony faded as she crept down the steep path, through the rocky canyon as she trailed her human quarry.

Montrose was already across their makeshift car park. His police cruiser was parked near a fallen pine, its petrified branches raking at the air around it. He was fumbling with his robes, trying to find the correct pocket that housed his keys. He was panicking and in shock after finally having to face the death he had been trying so hard to cheat. Annie dropped to a squat and advanced, sneaking from car to car, then bush to bush as she drew upon her victim. All that lay between them now was the fallen tree. She wanted to carve Donovan's name onto the bastard's heart. She'd gut him and force feed him his own entrails. She'd...

'Who's there?' Montrose called out, spinning around, raising his gun. Annie fell down low and hid from his eyeline below the bulk of the tree. She caught a glimpse of the gun as Montrose aimed it over the trunk. Had he reloaded? How many rounds were left in the pistol's chambers? She couldn't tell. He'd been behind her when he had fired at Connor, and after the first round was fired she had been deafened to a point where the other rounds had not registered.

'Kathleen?' he whispered, his voice low, but hopeful.

Annie began to crawl, making her way further up the tree and then picking her way over the trunk, through its leafless branches. Montrose was still looking back, towards the path to the quarry. Annie took her place behind the tail end of the cruiser and gripped the knife in two hands.

'Kathleen? We fucked up? Anyone there? We fucked up.'

He turned back to the car and placed the key into the lock. Lowering his gun.

Annie raised the knife and charged, swinging her arms around in a wide arc, striking him in the back. The blade sank deep and Montrose cried out as he span around, knocking Annie away, her fingers slipping from the knife, leaving it within him. Montrose panic fired, squeezing the trigger over and over. Only two shots came though, both of them wide of their mark. Annie got up and charged again, trying to tackle him but, outweighing her by over a hundred pounds, Montrose took the blow then responded with his own. Punching Annie square in the face with a straight right.

Blood gushing from her nose, Annie fell backwards. Montrose let out another haughty scream. Each movement was tearing the wound in his back open further and further and his eyes began to droop. She wasn't sure if she had hit anything vital or if the night's horrors had just taken their toll on him and he was ready to crash. Either way his hand still fumbled beneath his robes, looking for more ammunition for his gun.

Agony was blooming across her face and her head span, but the faces of her lost loved ones kept her focused and she barrelled towards Montrose again, and again he tried to stop her. However he was starting to slow, the pain and the blood loss taking their toll. He took Annie's full weight to the gut as she speared him, knocking him back, and he twisted and fell against the fallen tree.

A large branch erupted through his side just below his lungs bringing with it a spray of blood. He began to thrash and shake, but he was held in place. He coughed, his mouth turning red instantly. He tried to compose himself before attempting to once again reload his gun, but Annie simply kicked the revolver from his enfeebled grip.

He dropped his hands to his sides in submission and Annie fell back, leaning against the car, both of their chests heaving as they tried to calm their breathing, though that task was nigh impossible for Montrose. He coughed.

'So what now? You going to watch me bleed out or kill me?'

Annie walked over to a nearby branch and kicked it loose. She picked up the makeshift spear and levelled it at Montrose, ready to run it through his chest.

'I deserve this,' he said. 'I fucked up. Do it fast,'

Movement caught her eyes across the lot. A lumbering figure marching towards them. Drenched in blood, oozing wounds littering his body, and a pale death's head mask locked on them. Connor had finished off the rest of the zealots and had his sights set on mopping up the survivors.

Sanity took back control of Annie's senses and she dropped the stake and turned to the cruiser, opening the door and slipping the keys into the ignition. She was amazed with herself at how easy it was. Not once did she fumble or shake and the car started first time, engine rumbling healthily into life.

She pulled away just as Connor drew down on them, but the ghoulish killer paid her no heed and made a beeline straight for Montrose. She took one look back in the rear view mirror and heard the piercing screams drown out the car's engine. She'd leave them to it. Leave the valley to its own horrendous ends. She had driven this path before with her late Donovan. She began to laugh and cry and gibber madly as she drove back down to the campsite, and past it. She drove on, out of the valley and past the bar and diner that would join their siblings in being boarded up and left abandoned now that their owners were dead. She drove on into a new dawn, forever changed. Away from the mountains, away from the valley, away from the madness there and most importantly away from her dreams of ever, EVER setting foot in the woods again.

# Epilogue

Drawing his thumbs from the now empty sockets he gazed down at his handiwork. The sheriff continued to kick and twitch as he attempted to scream. The jellied remains of his eyes sluiced down his cheeks and past his silent mouth, as he'd torn his vocal cords almost as soon as Connor had started his work.

The killer watched on for a moment, contemplating his next move, then returned his thumbs to the gaping holes in Montrose's skull. He pushed harder until the back of the orbital cavity cracked inwards, driving shards of skull into the brain, finally killing the cult leader.

Connor rose again and turned his face to the moon. Light still refusing to reveal his true eyes.

Sight unseen he closed them and listened.

Past the sound of the waterfall he could hear the engine of the car fading fast into the night and within it, the thundering heartbeat of the girl who drove. She would be out of the valley long before he could stop her and on any other night it would have been sacrilege, an insult of the highest order, but he'd spilt plenty of blood already, caused enough pain.

As well as the engine he could hear the other cultists. The smart ones who had fled when he had appeared. He would hunt them down over the course of the next few days.

He left the corpse of Montrose and made his way back up to the quarry floor. The slaughter here had left the ground slick with blood. The bodies were strewn about, ravaged and desecrated. They had spilt his blood in order to sate the thirst of the ones they considered to be their masters, but none of them heard the call the way he did. None of them knew how to truly serve. He kicked one of the pretenders aside and found what he was looking for.

The idol.

He held it up to his face, the one he'd made from fabric and blood. The one he hoped mirrored the face on the statue well enough to show his devotion to it. He locked his dark eyes with those of the effigy and they stood in silent appreciation of each other. Their work had only just begun.

This was only the beginning.

CONNOR FINLAYSON WILL RETURN

# ABOUT THE AUTHOR

David Charlesworth is a horror author from Liverpool, England. The city is perhaps most famously known for giving the world Clive Barker, Ramsey Campbell and a band that swept the globe with their broad popularity and musical genius... "Dead or Alive".

He is a born and bred horror fan and was raised on George Romero films, the Friday the 13th franchise and most terrifyingly of all, the Inspector Gadget cartoon. He studied art and design in school and college until he realised that he couldn't draw and turned his hand to writing instead. He mostly works within the Splatterpunk subgenre of Horror, writing the slasher series, "Death Head Valley" but he also dabbles with "Cosmic Horror", despite being warned about the negative effects it can have on ones mental health.

He still lives in Liverpool and says he will never leave. His hobbies are writing, drinking and drinking. Though why you want to know is beyond him. What is this? A dating website?